I AM AINSLEY RUDOLPH
Always the woman but never the wife

A Novel

By

Melissa Cobb

Changing the Heart Publishing

Louisville, Mississippi

I AM AINSLEY RUDOLPH

Copyright 2022 by Changing the Heart Publishing

ISBN: 979-8-218-11620-0

LCCN: 2022051159

Printed in the United States

Moral:

Such is the way of an adulterous woman; she eateth, and wipeth her mouth, and saith, I have done no wickedness (Proverbs 30:20)

Words of Wisdom:

This story is dedicated to all the women and or men who are caught up in what someone else has going on. Be mindful when you discover the person's real situation and please listen to your gut instinct; for it knows when the heart doesn't.

INTRODUCTION

I go to bed dreaming about dicks, because I've had so many in my life. I always needed to feel something hard in me, besides the heart in my chest. Which brings the entirety of my existence to a sham, from being a diabetic, to dejection, and from anxiety to low self-esteem? I had no peace as a child. My parents kept up appearances behind closed doors, and I suffered. They didn't love or understand me. You can say it's because of the incest and fondling I endured from my mother's family. Sadly enough, my mother knew it. She stated for years, it was my fault for being beautiful and remarkably made, and I believed her until her and dad's divorce was final.

She says she was afraid of having a bad name on the family and believed I was strong enough to overcome being touched. She didn't count on the penetrating part of having a huge dick going in and out of my tiny virgin canal and ripping my anal cavity, by her brother. You don't know the happiness I had when her brother was put away for

1

sexually exploiting a minor as he did me at my tender age of seven through fifteen. Going through depression and rebellion made me change. Like many young adult women, I became wild, sexually active and doing all manner of drugs to feel good about life. Those actions caused me to try men and women alike; which all did me wrong.

These so-called loves made my outlook on love void and bleak. I could not find my own man, so I played around with married men, deacons, pastors, and men in relationships. These types of men were the best and the most desired, because all I had to do was be a text or a phone call away. My sole job was to be available for them and do what the women in their lives wouldn't do. The downside was, I still felt alone and used whenever the man went home to their real family; while, I easily aborted over five members of my family. However, I didn't want abortions, but they dared me to keep it. I couldn't afford it anyway and none of them wanted me to carry the child to term. I knew getting rid of the babies was in my best interest, all because they all didn't want their perfect-looking lives destroyed by me. It was funny how I was sloppy seconds and loved it.

I would pretend I was a friend, but that was all an allure. I know these men didn't want to lose the woman they love by being with someone they don't want a future with. Then I got pregnant with Jared, my first living child, by a deacon in our church. My twin sister Paisley, kept my son and what I made off my conquests, I gave to her for him.

A year later, I settled down with a man and gave up my cunning ways. He took me out to dinner, spent time with me, understood me, and made me feel special. These actions changed my lying life; therefore, I wanted to wait for sex. He didn't like it, but after months of dating me, he viciously raped me. Here my last son was conceived as a reminder of my choices. With a greater choice at hand, I had my tubes tied for fear of having more kids.

I refused to bring more children into this

world and not provide for them. Life already was hard, and having more mouths only added frustrations, stress, and depression. Don't get me wrong, I love my boys, but I am a promiscuous woman and a woman like me has desires and needs. With the realization that I am a mother, I got my son back from my sister and changed my mental state to do better. I refused to use my body as a ploy for men's enjoyment. I heard about Christ and thought HE was using me to bring marriages together. I discovered I didn't know HIM personally, at all. This eye-opener led me to church.

My life still did not improve as I struggled to make ends meet on a fixed income. There is a man out there for me. Surely, I can be loved, like the wives of the men whose bed I've shared. Life could not be this cruel to women who do their best with what they have. The many tears I cried could not stop me from playing with the idea of ending it all. I came to the point of destruction. I am lost in myself and the things I have gone through. My sons deserved better, and it pained me not being able to give them all they need. I didn't think about my life anymore. Things went downhill fast. Everything that could go wrong did go wrong. Jared's father quit paying child support and started working for cash, my SSI check was stopped because of paperwork they claimed to not have received, and HUD wasn't renewing my lease, all because their system error. The last straw was, they cut me off my EBT stamps, stating, I wasn't cooperating with the father of my child. The DHS claimed through DNA, Kyle's father wasn't his father, when I know who raped and impregnated me.

My children were suffering and in need of things to change and change quickly, if I am to make it. I prayed about it, and nothing happened. I've spoken with my sister Paisley about my life, but she did not get it. Her life was perfect and sheltered. She never went through what I did. My sister enjoyed life the way it was intended and never wanted for anything. The way she looked at me, I know she thought I brought this all on myself because of my bad choices. It's not like I woke up wanting to be the way I am. It's not like I didn't want or try to change. Thinking about my life, compared to my sister's, saddened me. I, on the other hand, felt worthless as a woman and hopeless as a provider. I was forced into thinking how everyone was waiting on me to give up. I woke up and knew the people's wait was over. I had enough as I cried from my soul. My life wasn't to be like this. Although I am very beautiful, persuasive, and caring, I was taught how to be crafty and how to prey on the weak. All I could not get on my own, my body got for me. I am a Rudolph, and Rudolph's don't get suckered into situations of pity and no self-worth. There was no way I could allow my children to be a burden on the state, nevertheless live in the custody of my mangled and twisted family.

With no more debating, I decided on drowning my children in the tub and hanging myself. As God is my witness, it all halted the day I found my only true love. Anthony walked into my life on the day I wanted to end my life. I met this church man on social media and by chance. He liked my picture, and I in boxed him to see if he knew me. I didn't know him, but I knew people attached to him. I searched all his social media pages and saw no wife or children. He never mentioned anyone special or close to him.

The man seemed nice. I felt I had nothing to lose; therefore, I told him my story. Surprisingly, he understood. This man did not judge me about my past or bad decisions. He listened to me as I poured myself out to him; a stranger. He stopped me from doing the unthinkable. This kind man showed compassion and was used by God to save me. He became an inspiration in more ways than one. Just the soundness in his voice opened my eyes to who I am as a woman, and how there is more to me than what I see. Sometimes on social media, he would post songs or scriptures for me to be encouraged about life.

He gave my fantasy a reality and made me believe in love and family. He helped me obtain my

GED, find better programs for my sons and me, took me places I needed to go, loaned me money I never gave back, and showed me genuine love. I know now real men exist in this cruel world. He changed my thought process in the middle of his mess. This man has time for my children and me. Nothing was off-limits for us, especially as him being my friend. Anthony showed the love and happiness I had been missing.

My spirit is different, and every day became a new lease on life for me. He listened in on my dilemmas and made sense when nothing else did. I don't know if it's the way we clicked because our childhoods were crappy. Either way, I was drawn instantly to what he was showing me. In my physiological mind, meeting Anthony was on time, to my present state.

Our chemistry synced, and I've never had it so well with any individual. A lot of times we talked about church and our day. He would give me what the Word says and how I could apply it to my life. It would work, and often, I would act like things weren't going right just for more of him. He would go more into the Word just for me. To get him off the church, I would ask how things were on his end as we finished each other sentences with a laugh. Being a listening ear made him open up about his circumstance. However, the little he let me in on allowed my heart to grow fonder. There were times he would be so angry and crying about his problems that it tore at my heart. It grieved me to the core about not being able to help him as he did me.

Sometimes I could read him so well, and other times I couldn't because of the shield of defense he used. Then, there were times he would confuse me and had me thinking all kinds of things about the possibility of other women in his life. We could be on the phone, and other women would call him. It made me jealous, because I had no idea who those women were. Then again, I didn't care as long as he was available for me and mine. But when he was unreachable, I'd reach further by showing him I understood the pain or discomfort. Me being there for him soothed him and did wonders for me. I made sense of his condition, and he knew it. Soon as he was calm, he'd tell me how much he appreciated me being there for him like no one ever has.

He is good to me, but that doesn't mean he is good for me, for I know gratitude is never needed if you are aware of your feelings. I truly desire and need him more than a woman like me should. Some parts of me want the old sly me to emerge, but I say I changed. I don't want to trick him into wanting me, but I find myself embedding him in my web of enticement by using suicide as a lure. He loves saving me, but I am pulling him under like an underwater current. He can't see himself drowning because, he sees me drowning. My attack kept him unfocused on his life and tuned into mine.

I shouldn't have time for foolishness; after all I'd been through. I shouldn't have time for a lot of things and falling in love shouldn't be one of them. My heart knows Anthony and I can have something special; I need him to see it as I do. I don't want to be a go-to girl or a standby anymore, then again, why not? My perception has gotten me into this fucked up situation. I need him in my life as bad as I need to breathe. I didn't think it was possible to love a man this much, but I do. I don't know his take on me or how he really feels, so I imagined it from the way he tenderly calls my name, comes by my house to see the boys and me.

I don't know if he is seeing anyone; for he never mentions a relationship and I never ask. My heart knows he is what I need and damn the others, if there are others. With a life of its own, those friendly feelings emerged into a strong connection; on my end a bond. This bond is the type of bond husbands and wives have. His voice penetrates me, and his presence draws me like water being pulled out of a well. He doesn't look at me in a relationship way, and that is what drew me. Anthony seduces my mind and feverishly appeals to my body. He overtakes my very thoughts, while the imagination rules many possibilities of us. I am thinking more and more of him and anxiously waiting for our talks. My every idea would be Anthony and his voice.

When he takes me to do errands, I make sure everything is on point. I would sexually brush my fingers against his to see him give a seductive smile; it did. I was leading him on, and he acted as if he was dumbfounded by my cunning ways. Making him mine had gotten into me as I flirted here or there with him. Like a man, he flirted back. It is obvious that men like a woman who pays attention to them. One day when we talked of sex. I told him I been fucked all types of ways and in different positions, but I hadn't ever been made love to and I wondered would it be real. He said, "You've had the wrong me taking you, but if a real man takes you, I promise you would know it."

My mind roamed the Anthony opened the door and asked in a hypnotic tone, "Where my pussy at?"

The word pussy made my pussy thump to reply. I laughed at him and said, "She here waiting good dick, she hasn't gotten wet in a while, so the dick might not be able to handle the water."

"I never met a horse I couldn't ride. I mean a pussy I couldn't fuck," his teasing reply made me squirm.

Since he said those words to me, there was no turning back. The line was crossed and, heavy dreams of him in the bed were all I thought about. Tasting him overtook any friendship we had left. Not trying to, but the old me was rebirth with a purpose. I became underhanded, seductive, conniving, and scheming on every level. I realized he couldn't see how I drew him in my love trap or the way I would play him.

Just because I could, I would call him all times of night in need of direction, because he said I could lean on him anytime for anything. He didn't lie. He would answer me and calm the lie I made up. There had been times I appeared unstable for him to rush over. When he arrived, I had him waiting for over an hour to see if he would be patient. The bad girl in me needed to see how long he would wait for me, because no man had.

I was trying to see if I was just as important as those other women he talked to on the phone. I needed to know how or if he would jump if I pulled his chain. I was tired of falling for all the wrong men, only to be let down. From that day, he became a man of his word. This supportive man is unconditionally always there. To prove this, I would back off. When he didn't hear from me, he would come after me sounding concerned and caring. Anthony either couldn't see my ploys or didn't care because of things in his life. He has told me about a friend of his, who thought less of our friendship.

He also claims to defend me and go against all anyone just for little ole me. A man has never defended me and to know he did, made him more irresistible. No matter what I said, did, or thought, he always had my side. I could count on him to talk to me or be by my side, no matter what. The way he and I act proves we make each other happy. Gladness became obvious for me having a man I could call at will. Regardless of what I asked, he never let me down. If I couldn't feed my kids, he came through with food or money. Because I couldn't drive, he took me everywhere I needed from the doctor's office, school, or grocery store. I even acted like I was broke so he would loan me money for household items, which I never paid back.

The kicker was family. I offered him to be the godfather to my sons because Anthony longed to be a father. He stated, "He could not because he didn't want false hope." I didn't get it. Whatever my boys needed, he got it for them without exchanging a word. Once when they both were sick, he came over and stayed all night with them. He acted like they were his, and they enjoyed him just as much. He would read and play with them like a real father. He would give them money for being good or buy them a happy meal or toy. I know I couldn't keep coming at him strongly so, I would back off here and there, just enough for him to miss me. It worked, but it hurt me to stay away, so I would give in and we would pick up as if time stood still for us.

Some days, our conversation would be personal, and some days it's platonic. It has been months since I had a man, and the cat and mouse game is wearing thin. However, when. I got out of character; he picked me up and pulled me into his world. He showed me his old community, introduced me to his friends, and showed me where he lived. The house was beautiful, and the atmosphere was family oriented. I imagined my boys and me with him at his grand house. With that in mind, I found myself throwing sexual hints or just hints of a future more his way.

Many a day I would say, "On a good day, Anthony, I like to go long and deep into the woods, just to jump in the water naked. The water would trickle down my breasts just enough to wet me. Do you know how good that would feel, Anthony, be soaking wet like that?"

He would laugh and say, "Girl, you wild, but I would enjoy seeing the water overtake you like that anytime because you would be stress-free."

One day, the conversation got real. He came at

me first by making smacking sounds and said, "Do you know what that sound is?"

My pussy already knew but my top mouth said, "No."

"This is me soaking my face in your pussy. Keeping your scent and not brushing my teeth."

After months of lying and pretending, he has finally taken the bait. To be blunt, my words were, "You can eat the bottom out of this pussy if you want to claim it as yours, for now."

"If you not letting any other man feast on you, I'll lick each lip, and tongue the middle," he responded sexually, as he laughed.

Laughing more, I would reply, "If you see me with a man, I promise it will be my husband. I'll charge it to the game if there is another woman. I know you are a damn good man, and I know women are always calling you because they call you when we are on the phone. I think you are making me jealous because you are jealous of me. I think you are playing with my mind on some sick level, because you know I need real love. I've been loyal to you when you had nothing. I have been by your side through all the things you had been dealing with, even if it wasn't as much as mine. I have been there for you. What are we to do? I can't keep giving my time to a man who may have a woman, because when I love, I love hard."

Lastly, he replied, laughing, "When I had nothing? When we love, we love. We have a bond. I have been there for you. What is best for us to do? I have been by your side through everything. I got you. I am here for you. I do love you, Ley."

He's finally aware of his feeling for me and, also giving him thoughts of us and the sex we could have. Then I tried him by saying, "Where you got to be for a couple of hours?"

"Nowhere."

"My sister has my boys. Let's go to my place."

He drove me there, and we went inside. The first part of the night, he couldn't get it up. The dick would not get hard, which frustrated me. The excuse was how he wasn't sure if he wanted to cross the lines of losing me as a friend. I explained the line was crossed when he took off his clothes and laid in the bed with me. Touching me with ease, he went under the covers, parted my legs. I inhaled as I waited for the first lick. Being seasoned in oral sex, he tasted me to perfection. My legs trembled so; I could not keep them on his shoulders. My man did a spectacular job at making me cum fast and hard. However, his penis still didn't rise. He felt ashamed. I assumed he didn't want me, but he said that was not it.

To give him comfort, I told him we don't have to have penetrating sex. My heart was lying because I wanted his dick in me, and I was devastated when it didn't work. A few more weeks passed and I called him over one night while the boys were gone. He rushed over as usual. When he came in, I was ready, and he understood what I didn't have to explain. His body followed me to my bedroom, on the left. This time the dick stood up and turned me out. It was passionate and fulfilling. He wasn't ashamed to be with me like other men were. After that one night, we were fucking with no condom all the time. In the car, at my place, on the side of the road, in his friend's vehicle, and everywhere we could when sexual feelings came.

My pussy never got dry because he always had his dick or head in it. Most of the time, he entered anal with no Vaseline, but my butt was wet anyway. I stayed ready for him and all he had to offer in the bed. It was weird knowing how he could only fuck me after he ate my pussy. When he did eat it, he ate my pussy so much I thought it was his favorite meal. He kept me weak and exhausted so that I didn't want anyone or anything but him. His dick wasn't all that; I have had bigger and better, but I loved him, and that made his dick the best.

He should have known I loved him when my pussy would suck him in every time he tried pulling out. She didn't want him to leave either. Most of the time, he only tasted me. I would ask him why only oral sex. He would say he wants to satisfy me and how it gives him happiness. I wanted to suck him, but he wouldn't let me. He told me he didn't want me to do it just yet because if I did him, I know for

20

a fact I was going to be there in his life forever. He would further explain how sucking dick was personal for him. He was making sure I was ready for all the love he has for me. Little did he know I was ready, the day he saved me and every day after our conversations involved.

My children were no longer a factor. I was head over heels in love with him. I know he feels the same way because of how he treats me; how he takes his time in bed with me. He would come over all the time and talk. Anthony would even ask my opinion on things concerning his life, then eat my pussy or fuck me from the back. He was taking care of me on every level possible. He would get a new vehicle and come show it off to me. This man would take me riding all over town then, I would ride him in my bed all night. I hate it when he closes his eyes though, I want them opened and focused on me. Focused on the only one who is pleasing him and would do anything for him as long as I had him.

Now is the time, I wished I didn't have my

tubes tied or a missing uterus. I could have a child, and we would be complete. My boys would have the father they needed, and I would have the man I deserve. That didn't matter, as long as he was sleeping with me. Life was looking up for me on every level. Again, I was on point whenever I was with him. He would kiss my lips tenderly and has told me he loved me. He told me how he didn't want to go back to his boring home and wished I could be there. That day, my heart skipped a beat, and I was getting the full benefits of a woman having her own family. He played with my children, and when they went to bed, he played with me. On Saturday nights, he would come over and spend hours with me and leave about 2 a.m. because he said that's a decent time a man must go home.

There is no way he has a woman by all the time he is giving my sons and me. When I call him, he answers and is more than ready to give his advice and time. We would talk on the phone off and on for hours all day, every day sometimes. We would laugh and share dreams and even speak of how we would like our life to change. I never knew sharing so much of me would let me in on so much of him. I knew another side of Anthony that made me desires him more. I knew what real love between a man and a woman could be like, minus the sex, but I can't lie; it is a bonus.

Sometimes he would tell me of other women calling him, and he tells me they need his advice or coming by to see him. I would feel a type of way because other women were getting his attention. I shouldn't be jealous, but I could not help it. I can't help the way I am feeling about my best friend. I see that now, and I know he should see this too. If he doesn't see it, then he's either waiting on me or waiting to see before he makes his move.

On a Saturday, he spent all day with us barbecuing, or I cook him dinner. He is my friend. He is my voice in the night. He is my love, and I never wanted him to leave, but he must go to church the next day. He has told me how he wants to take the boys and me to church service with him one day. It was family time, my time, in my eyes. We laughed more than anything, and that made time with him everything. He would pay my rent or give me money to help me, for he knew my struggles. On Valentine's Day, he would come over with baskets of goodies for me and the boys. Sometimes he would come over, and we chilled with no sex, but that was seldom. Anthony took time for me. He does everything just right, and I have no reason to doubt him.

CHAPTER 1

My life was put to a halt and short-lived the day I answered the phone and heard, "Ley, I must tell you something."

It was the voice of my love. It made me nervous as he said, "How can I start this off?"

"How about from the beginning?" I replied nervously.

"I know God is not pleased with me and how I have been acting."

"Why would you say that? You have been everything I need you to be. I love you. The boys love you. No matter what we need, you provide."

"Yeah, but the truth is, I don't have any children, and your children gives me joy; but I am married. I have been unhappily married for two years now."

Now, I didn't know he's married, and I didn't feel the need to question him about his life, because his life and my life did not coincide. Many questions were on me like, what man is always available for a single woman like me? How could he be married with all the time he spends around my children and me? Where is his wife? My voice left me. I screamed, "Married!"

"Yeah, I'm married to a doctor."

"Why didn't you fucking tell me before I loved you with my heart and soul?"

"Would it have mattered? Would it have mattered if I had a wife or not?" he replied slowly in a calm manner.

He made a valid point. It probably wouldn't have mattered much, but it would have mattered some. I've been involved in marriages on more than one occasion. I called myself straying from that lifestyle, but I found myself back in it and caught off guard. He said, "The need became irrelevant because my wife trusts me, and she believes me. I've known her before she was even in medical school. I told her about you. I didn't tell her how important you and your friendship were to me. I kept it personal, because I am to console you. It wasn't supposed to be like this."

"Be like what?" I asked with a teary voice.

"Love?" I heard sweetly.

"Love? Love who!" I yelled.

"Is it possible to love two women the way I love you and my wife?" he questioned.

I could only respond, "You will love one and care for the other. Whichever one you love would be the one who has your heart."

"Ainsley, I know we are special friends and have done a lot of good things out of character, but I believe I am in love with you and just love her. The thing is, no matter how good it is with you, I can't and won't ever leave my wife. I am not going anywhere and I won't let her leave me. She is the one who truly has my heart. You and the boys will always have a small portion of my heart."

"What about how I feel? Have you considered what this could be doing to me? You knew how I felt about married men because of the lifestyle I lived. You knew I had trust issues and you knew how I fell for you. You could have turned me down at any time, or left me the Hell alone and I would have been okay with that. But he you kept talking to me, even flirting with me. You made me change the rules of my heart."

"I did and, so did you. You grown. You knew the games you were playing with me. Use this time, right now to let me know how you feel?" he asked.

Trying to be honest, I replied, "I feel we can have something great. I believe we have a strong bond that's unbreakable, unchangeable, infallible in this relationship, and we can overcome this marriage. Since you came into my life, my soul had a new lease. You are my soul mate, and I am yours. What we have is not a mistake, or maybe God put me in your life for a reason. Whatever it is, I think I am the inspiration for whatever is going on. I need you. God knows I need you."

"You aren't an inspiration for whatever is going on. God is not the author of confusion, and I should have known better, but my flesh got the best of me." He paused, and then spoke intimately, "Talking to you, seeing you, touching you and yes, tasting your sweet-smelling pussy lips is something

28

I won't ever forget."

With light tears in my voice, he heard,
"Maybe I am to experience this kind of love to
know it still exists, but I have found all this love in
you. We are so much more than what I thought, but
you are married."

He asked in disbelief, "Am I not worth your
time because I am an unhappy married man?"

Trying to make him believe me, I spoke,
"Anthony, you can't be worth my time, even if you
understand me and profoundly, we are destined for
greatness. Sometimes I get you, and sometimes I do
not. Sometimes you let me in your world,
sometimes you do not. No other man has made me
feel like you do, and I've had numerous lovers. I do
not want another man. Anthony, you are a dear part
of me, and you will always be the love of my life."
He was quiet. So I spoke with positivity, "I am
going to sit back and see where all this is going.
You have me even if she wants to be stupid. I will
ride this out with you until the end. I'll wait for you
because I believe in us."

thing you told me was suicide is not the answer. You told me I would end up in Hell because I am in my right mind and know better. You even said suicide is a selfish act, but in honesty, I may kill myself and take the boys with me."

He was quiet. Knowing him like I believe I do, he was shaking his head and trying to think. Finally, he spoke with remorse, "I can't take that if you did a thing like that. You have your whole life ahead of you and to do something like that would break me down. You would be robbing those who love you out of loving you. It's the thought of not having you living and being with me and the boys. Please understand. You and the boys are a very important part of me. I can still be in their lives and yours as a friend if you still want me to, long as you know I am willing to just be a friend and play my marriage by ear. Then again, I need peace in my home, and being your friend disrupts any peace I have. I have a wife and I must respect her before you and your boys. It's true. Hadley is getting on my everlasting nerves with her never-ending questions about me and you, but at the same time I don't want to mislead you either. My heart is fond of you, and you doing something like that would haunt me forever. Ley, please don't."

"You aren't misleading me. You are the only one who loves me. If I rob anyone, it would be you, but I am grown and so are you. If you are still my friend and encouraging me to be the best I can be nothing else matters. For you, I would continue to live this life, but I don't want to do it without you in it. I can't lose you at all, Anthony, and I don't want confusion in your home. But I need you! Right now, our love for each other is exposed. There is no turning back for us. We just haven't pursued it. I will take you being a friend over not having you at all. Tell me this. How are you to be my friend and not want to be anything more?"

"I won't act on my feelings because I know me. I am a married man to a woman I have always loved. It would hurt her if I was with you and I never want to cause her any pain. There have been times, you captured my complete attention and I neglected seeing what made me love her in the beginning. I found myself staring at you and wondering what it would be like to be your husband and her lover?"

"But you have said once before how you love me, and you will protect me. Now you say you love me; but can't leave her. Which is it, because I am confused?"

"I know of my feelings. I wish you had met her first and I was the tag along. She is like you but smarter in a sense. She didn't have a hard life, but it wasn't that great. Hadley knows the game while you had to learn the game. She is loyal and far from stupid, while you are loyal and have been stupid. She can be like a mother hen about those she loves, and I am what she loves dearly. Before you came along, we were all we had. We have gone through so much turmoil and nonsense that we made it. Although she doesn't cook or clean to my high expectations, I wasn't a good husband or provider to her either. She has never been unfaithful to me, and she isn't my type, but with all her flaws and crazy ass ways, she has always been damn good to me. She has set the bar high in my life for any bitch to jump. The things she has done for me in my life, I can't ever repay or list. Whatever I need, she gives it. The times she should have given up on me she stayed. I am imperfect for her, but she is what I need. Leaving her is the last thing I would do. I will fall apart without her. She makes no sense, but she is sense. You get it?"

"I do and you know I do," I spoke with tears.

"Ley, I know it can't be more than what we have. I know it is not fair to my wife to fall for you, but that's where we at right now. My wife says you are a Jezebel demon out of Hell."

"What's that?" I asked with a teary smile.

"An evil spirit sent to cause havoc in our lives and go on. She believes you only want to destroy what we have left of our marriage, then go about your business to leave us to pick up the pieces and try to mend us back over again."

"You believe it? You think I am this

Jezebel?"

"Sort of but let me explain. According to
Deliverance and Warfare, one part of a Jezebel
spirit is a woman who is without a husband,
adulterous, and licentious. This type of woman is
characterized by domination, control, and
manipulation. She doesn't care who is being hurt
for her. She only wants what she wants. Now if I
give you my attention, she doesn't get any. Since I
have been talking to you, I don't talk to her. I argue
and get mad at her, just to talk to you. Honestly, I
know she knows what she is talking about, but I
downplay her and keep you at bay. She has
described you and never saw you. She has dreamed
of your apartment furniture and where I sit while I
am there. She is right, and that is why I can't let you
keep getting close to me like this. It must stop. My
marriage is breaking and it's out of my control. In
my confusion, you are what sane is."

"You think you can stop talking to me, stop
thinking about me, stop thinking about all the ways
you take me and stop wanting me for all the right

reasons?" I asked him.

"I can't, but I must. Do you know how hard it is for me to lie to her? She sees right through me, and I know she feels it because she calls me out on it. It breaks my heart about the pain in her face, and the crying she does hurts me. It tears at my heart to deceive her. Sometimes if we disagree about you, she cries out to God. I know He is hearing her. I just don't know what He is going to do about it on her behalf. Sometimes I think she will give in, get angry and do what she thinks I am doing, but she doesn't. If she becomes hell bent on hurting you, nothing but God can stop her. She knows better, but after all I've put her through, she won't do better. I know she won't. You and the boys should not be a part of her fury because of what I have done to her."

"What about me and the tears you are going to make me cry if we are not special friends? You said you would always be there for me and now you are speaking differently. You are confusing me, and I don't get it. I need you in my life like we need air to breathe. I need to know you are here for me, through this mess." I sobbed uncontrollably with exaggeration.

"I can't promise that like I want to. From the disagreements that I've had with my wife, I believe she will do damage to you and me both. I never meant for any of this. Believe me, you have a place in my heart and only you and I know about it. I hate you are being affected as much as I hate Hadley is hurting because of our so-called friendship. I am tired of hurting my wife because I desire your presence. I don't want things to be more than what she already thinks."

"Well, what she thinks is not true. In my eyes, we haven't done anything wrong! She is the one wrong! She is jealous of nothing. She has everything and I don't have anything. Your wife is taking you from me and I don't like it! I need you, Anthony Vaughn! I don't want to be without any part of you!" I kept saying through my many tears.

"You think me loving you is not more. You think Hadley is wrong because of how we are feeling towards each other?"

"I'm saying, what about our friendship? We are more than sex and I don't care to talk about her, because of her, I am crying out my soul."

"I know my wife. She will sue you for that alienation of affection thing."

"What is that?"

"If she has proof of an affair," he spoke, but I cut him off.

"We aren't having an affair! You know that! You have touched my heart and soul in more ways than one."

"This is an affair and I'm taking affection from her and giving it to you and the boys. I am not making it work like I should, because of you. I am talking to you more than I am her. I spend more time with you and the boys than I do with her. I do for you quicker than I do her. I already sinned all the times I started thinking of you more than I should. So how is that not an affair, if my affair starts in conversation with you long before the bedroom?"

"No! We are there for each other and it

constitutes not an affair in my book. You give me the Word of God and you instruct me on how to live a better life. You complete me."

"Ley, an affair can consist of more than just sex. If I feel any other way about any other woman other than my wife, that is an affair. The feelings I give you are solely meant for Hadley, but you have crept into my life like the wind, and a part of me don't want you to stop blowing. You make me feel good. You make me feel like a man who has a woman that needs him. Hadley doesn't need me, as you all do."

"Well, that's her fault if she doesn't understand or listens to you. She should be there for you like a real wife should. This woman you married doesn't see how great of a man you are. She is not letting you make your own mistakes. She guards you like you are a child, and you aren't, Anthony. You can have your friends. You don't need her telling you what to do. She should be focused on making things work with you and not wondering what we are doing. We have this over

42

here."

"She is my wife and she's not there because she works. I understand her job pays the bills and it helps me help you when I don't have it. I just don't like it. Ley listen, I'm giving you a heads up. She can sue you in the right state. She can and will make your life pure hell, all because of what I've done. I know her. You don't. Sure, Hadley is sweet and caring, but she can be a very cold-hearted, cruel and evil bitch. She will make you and your boys suffer and go through all types of mess because she has the money to do it and won't stop until she does it. I can't have her doing that to you and the boys. You have been through enough already. What she can do would throw you over the edge. If you have never seen the rage of a scorn woman, you've never met my wife."

"I can apologize to her for trying to be a pest in your marriage. I can tell her I'm sorry for any problems I may have caused her, but I believe God sent you to me and for me to help rebuild your marriage in some way."

He completely ignored me as he sternly said, "Don't you talk to my wife. Don't say shit to her. I told you, she isn't stupid by a long shot and is not one to play with. She figures out puzzles and most importantly, she prays."

"I'm just trying to help. I don't want you to leave me alone because she doesn't know how wonderful our bond is. She can't imagine living a life like mine and having someone like you come into it, just to leave!"

"I can't have a bond with you and one with my wife. It doesn't work like that. It's a different relationship and a different level. No one will ever have my heart but her. I don't care how jacked up her thinking is. She's mine. I'm the one messing that up. Ley, I can't stop her if she has vengeance because she has that long bread."

"So, because she has money, I don't have any part of your heart. Is that what you are telling me?"

"I'm saying I don't give a damn. I'm not leaving my wife."

"You always tell me the word. Tell me something right now to ease the pain I feel in my heart."

He was kind of quiet. I heard him breathe on the phone as he said, '1 Peter chapter four verse eight: And above all things have fervent charity among yourselves: for charity shall cover the multitude of sins.' Whatever or however, you feel, love will cover it. You must be on fire with love for your fellow man. You must believe love will conquer all things despite of all things."

"I believe you, Anthony. If you tell me love covers sin; then love covers sins point blank."

The phone was quiet as he added, "Her ultimatum was if I continue being your friend, she will destroy you and everything connected to you. I know all you've been dealing with. I can't let her do that. I told her I would leave you alone, so she will leave you alone."

My heart busted as Anthony hung up the phone.

CHAPTER 2

For many months, he did not contact me, and my boys kept asking about his return. I had no answer. I kept calling his cell phone, his house phone and talking to his friends for any information. I was a mental wreck as well as angry. It matters not to me if he is married. It's essential we remain friends. Because I vowed to be in his life at any cost and right now it is costing me my heart and my sanity. It took him leaving me alone to realize how much I really do love him. He crosses my mind and I cry. He is my soul mate and life. I found myself in a depressed state, with no one. Anthony was all I had and because of his non-caring, always jealous ass wife, I don't have him.

I don't have his smile, his gentle hand, and his caring words. I'm heartbroken and in love to sum it up. Anthony is my dream comes true. God created him just for me and I know the Lord has brought me into his life for a reason. I know God doesn't make mistakes like our chance meeting, and then take him away. My Lord is not unrighteous enough in any aspect, but the Lord did that to me.

My thoughts became desperate and deceitful for Anthony. I summed it up; he belongs with me and my boys. I sent word by people who knew him and that didn't work. I tried him numerous of times, but he blocked me on all social media, messages, Face Time and calls. I even requested ten dollars through Cash App, just to see if he would respond, and he didn't.

To be more desperate as I already am, I started going to his church. The ushers would take my sons to Anthony's Sunday school class. They loved it and I know he loves having them. I would listen to the preacher tell me stuff I've heard Anthony say before. They would come home and tell me he said this and that. My boys would tell how Anthony asked about me and to tell me hello. Still no wife and I really didn't care. The people didn't make me feel uncomfortable and that too did not matter. Whatever I could get, my objective was the same; Anthony.

On this day, he brought his class out front to

answer questions about the Bible. I saw him and melted as he flashed that smile. I felt butterflies in my stomach. This man with so much power over me but he won't talk to me. When I got home, I sulk at the fact that he is really gone. I am miserable beyond fixing. I went on social media stating, I need a friend to talk too, then the day after church my phone rang. I didn't recognize the number. Going against my judgment I said, "Hello."

The line was quiet. Then I heard, "This is Hadley Vaughn, Anthony's wife and I normally don't make house calls, but you calling my house has gone too far. He says he has told you to leave him alone, and you won't. If he wants you, he can have you, but he doesn't. Today I'm telling you to leave us alone. Warning comes before destruction. Get over whatever he had with you, while you still can."

My heart beats rapidly because she is calling me about the man we both love. I said, "I hadn't heard from Anthony. The last time we talked, he told me he is married."

"Hell yeah he married and you better quit contacting him. That means all contact! Do you know how stupid you look going to our church, panting over a man who will get you and your boys hurt?"

"You need to tell him that. He used to call me just as much, all day, every day. Church is a free place, and does he know you are talking to me and why can't you get over it? He is a man and if he contacts me, I'm contacting him back."

Her tone changed as she said, "You are not the only one and it is okay to be in love with my husband. He is a great guy and it's easy to fall for him, but if you continue this with him, you will only be hurting yourself. On Judgment Day, you will stand before a just God and my husband won't be standing there with you. I'm trying to stop this now, before it gets out of hand. You have no idea what you are getting into and because of your naïve spirit; I'm overlooking your tone."

Speaking truthfully and with no feelings, I told her, "For a while I didn't think he was your husband because he always with me. Where were you when he needed you? I've been there for him, and you weren't around. I was there when he didn't have anything."

"Wait. When did he not have anything? I make sure he has it all and then some. Who cares where I was or about what you think? I've always been there for him. Right now, I'm making sure you know he is my husband, and I am warning you. I won't warn you again, little girl."

"Don't threaten me!"

With no anger or disrespect in her tone, her words were firm. "I don't make threats. I make promises, and today I just got fed up with you and him. While your kids were at your sister's house, I was coming to your house, but you answered the phone. Look at God."

Giving her the entire attitude I could muster, I spoke. "Guess I better come after you first. I know where you live. It's nothing for me to come at you and take you out."

"Best believe I have a boat load of ass. To

get some ass, bring some ass and I'll pull up at your front door. Word of mouth, if I don't send for you, don't come for me."

"But you still with him and you coming at me" I stated to his wife.

"The devil I know is better than the devil you don't."

Snapping to Anthony's defense, I yelled, "You don't know anything about the man you don't be with. He has been everything but a devil."

"And you want to be with the man you don't know anything about. Little girl, he lies to you, and he lies to me. Get fucking real, get off the system and get your sick diabetic ass a job. Make yourself available to single men; that's if you can find one that wants all the heavy baggage you have. Let me know if you feel the same way when it's all said and done. You ain't got shit but a conversation and that gets bored."

"You don't know anything about me or what all I been through! But for you to be on my line, your husband must want me."

"I'm trying to save you, but I see now you don't want to be saved. I know more than you think I do, and you foolish if you don't think my husband don't talk to me. You really think he believes I am all that bad, but he is still with me?" She sounded sincere.

"If I am doing anything, it's because he is letting me."

"What is he letting you do now? Not a damn thing! Know your place and stop trying to get in mine," she threatened.

"That's not hard to do. You leave him unattended too much and if you were doing what you needed to do, you wouldn't be having what you think is a problem with me," I told his wife.

"I don't have problems, you do. I have situations. You want my husband. I don't want anything from you, not even those raggedy ass bastard kids. So glad you got your tubes tied. You should have had your uterus taken out. We don't need any more bullshit floating walking around stanking up other people's lives."

"Say what you will about me. You don't talk about my damn kids! Bitch, have you some, so your husband won't play father figure to mine."

"I called you to warn you, not to tongue wrestle. I have a career and a life. I took time out my busy schedule to help your needy ass out. Trust me I am helping you out."

"I see your help doesn't include your husband," I spat.

Hadley laughed at me like I was stupid. "He is married, and you will always be in some wife's shadow. Don't you get tired of always being the woman who "cums" last?"

"I believe God brought me in his life for a reason. Maybe for you both to come closer together, realize you need each other and for me to see love; not to break you up."

"Who dropped you on your head for you to think God would cause division in a marriage? You don't even respect yourself and to think I'm trying to warn you."

"I don't need your warnings and I have lost all respect for you," I stated in a distasteful way.

"Ha! You lost respect for me the day you fell for my husband. Right now, you are waiting on the perfect opportunity to snare him in a web. You playing, I'm eating and he bullshitting you."

"I tell you what. I will show you a bitch and give you something to talk about, because Anthony and I will always be friends!" I screamed at his wife.

"Your friendly ass can do what the hell you think you got to do, and my married territorial ass will do what the hell I need to do. You are not his first rodeo, regardless of what he tells you. Join the circus you clown. Ley, you will always be the woman but never a wife. You can't wear the shoes of this boss bitch."

She hung up and my hands shook. My brain can't believe what just took place. Anthony told me not to talk to her and I did. I became dizzy.

demanding. In truth, I repositioned myself for teasing him. I could not let him back out. Anthony removed himself from my grasp and extended his hand. I touched it and he snatched me up closer to him. He made my body cover his. He stepped back and looks me up and down. I became bashful.

"You don't ever need to be ashamed. You are beautiful, and tonight I want all of you; although, I am unsure."

I know he is another woman's husband, but tonight none of that matter. I don't care if it matters. The mood is right, and he is easy prey for me and taking advantage of him won't be a big problem. Anthony is where he needs to be and tonight, I truly need him to be in love with me; even if it's for a moment. This man of mine lifted me up and carried me in my bedroom like a groom does his wife on a honeymoon.

As if I were weightless, he placed me on the bed beside him. I didn't know what to do as he made me desire him. These new actions frightened me, but I welcomed it. I'm much unprepared for him and this. He rose up on his elbow and spoke with doubt, "I know this is wrong, but we feel so right. God only knows what I am thinking right now."

I saw his change in demeanor and thought quickly. "Anthony, leave God out of this. Do whatever you want without consequences. You are alone, and it won't be wrong to be with me like this. You need someone tonight and I need you tonight, if it's only for the night. I've waited a long time to have you, but I don't want you pressured into sleeping with me again. I know I love you and I would do anything just to have you, if you will have me just this once. I promise, you won't regret giving yourself to me."

"I know how I am feeling right now, and I know we have crossed the line."

Anthony lifted his hand to embrace the nipple on my breast. His finger trace alone gave me chills. He glared down at me as his fingers lightly squeezed my nipple. I forced words out of my mouth. "Don't think of it as us crossing the line. Think of it as a man and a woman who needs to not be alone right now. Let me show you how a woman makes love to a man she says and knows she loves."

I made that statement as I let a tear drop. I know he hates seeing me cry and I know it does something to him. Anthony wiped my tear and kissed me completely. Her husband is weak to me, and I truly know it. His wife can think however she feels, I am the one her man is going to nut in. I am the one who is going to fuck him. A smile overwhelmed me as he plucked at my breast. I moved away from him. Anthony pulled his clothes off where he laid.

The sight of his manhood made me weak. I

motioned to taste him, but he said, "No. I can't let
you do it just yet."

That statement kind of dampened the mood.
I knew then, he wouldn't let me do what he thinks is
a special thing. I didn't like it, but I planned to put
that dick in my mouth and that will be something
more special for us. I went over to the table and got
a few of those strawberries in my hand. Anthony
watched as I bit into the strawberry sexually.
Making my move, I climbed into the bed although I
didn't know what to do. I am nervous and excited,
but sure of being with him.

I placed myself beside him and kissed all
over him. The scent of his skin doesn't need
cologne. The very idea of this man made me wet. I
didn't know how I'd contain myself, but I must
make this good. Anthony said, "Ah."

Peeping through my eyes, I saw his were
closed. I eased further and further down his lean
captivating body. My arm purposely bumped the
dick stalk. It swayed and tempted me to do the
tasting better than that bitch he married. Not caring
but being overtaken with lust, my strawberry-filled
mouth found his penis. He spoke softly, "No, Ley."

But I took his no for yes and kept on licking
on him as I swallowed the fruit. He kept saying,
"Ley, baby no."

I am more turned on by him saying no. This
time, I put the entire man stick in my mouth as I

swallowed the last red delight. My man placed his hands on my head and rocked his dick in my mouth. Moving my head to see his toes wiggling, my love kept repeating like a chant, "Shit, Ley. I didn't know."

I had him. He didn't want me to do what I think his wife has never done. I knew if I put my fire-hot breath on him, he wouldn't be able to help himself. I knew he would not stop until I had him fully erected in my mouth. Being a careful dick sucker, I teased and toyed on his nice sized balls. This man is truly blessed below his waist, I thought. My tongue licked him from the head to the base, going in a circular motion. Anthony was misbehaving and to make him know it's me, I claimed my stake. "Anthony, this is my dick tonight, and tonight I fuck you the way I want and the way you need."

He could only nod in agreement. I used my right hand to hold the stout stem. In my view was a pure shiny mushroom cap. Taking the pearl clamp out of my hair, I placed it in my mouth and went out of control. I caused him excitement. Then I stopped and got up. I stood on the bed and towered over him. Anthony smiled at me as I turned away from him, closed my legs to sit on him backwards. We both made a sound of static as his penis pierced my soul from below. I wanted to melt like butter in a hot pan. I was unable to move. Soon as Anthony placed his hands on my hips, I eased up off him and knew having him inside me is where he needed to be. Using his legs as my sturdy handles, I went up and down on him with class.

In this position, I made sure he had a great view as he watched my ass clap each time on his dick head was almost out of me. Because of my model figure and nice round ass, jockey styling him and teasing wasn't hard. This is too awesome, but I wasn't thinking about me. I must make it good to him. He is the only thing I cared about and to keep him wanting me, I must out-do the wife. There is no other way around it. My pussy is on point and soon enough, my head game will be strong for him.

However, this man beneath me did not let me move. Anthony became demanding as he tightened his grip on my hips to keep me in place. He doesn't want me fucking him, I thought. Either way, he pounded me from below like an oil worker drilling for oil, in a strange place. I cared not for his rapid pace, but this man's every stroke was on point. He is a skillful lover and a challenging one at that. But role playing has never been my thing. He kept calling me a bitch and I didn't like it, but he does. To switch things up, I stopped moving and jerked up off him. He said, "What's wrong?"

"Nothing is wrong. I want you to dog fuck me."

With his dick bouncing sturdy, he got up

and shook it a few times. I got on my back and made my feet touch my shoulders. He inserted all five of his fingers inside me and massaged my vagina happily. He's making sure I am ready, I thought as he did it a few times. His tempo was faster as he jabbed my pussy with anger. A brief second later he stopped and said, "I want big fruits in this pussy's mouth."

I didn't understand. He kept his eyes fixed on me while my pussy made a Sunday dinner spread. He placed four of the five bananas on top of each other and pierced my moist vagina. The task was hard for me. I could take it if he's gentle, but he wasn't. Anthony not only jammed and rammed, but he shoved the hard green unripe fruit inside me with vengeance. I don't know if he likes it like this, but he is not the one feeling it. I closed my eyes to the pain and thought, if he wants kinky sex I am going to give it to him better than anyone.

Anthony finished the physical hand torture by pulling the sticky fruit out and throwing it on the floor. I was glad. I asked, "You want to taste it or you going to play in it?"

"I'm going to fuck it."

"I can handle it. Make sure you can handle it."

Anthony got on top of me and entered me harshly. I swore I felt his dick in my throat. He is very deep in me. I am already in a position where I can't move and him getting nothing but pussy is a lot. My friend, my lover, is all in me with his eyes closed and making his mouth go opposite sides of his stride. He is rocking my body in a mad way. I kept saying louder, "You can't nut! This dick ain't shit!"

The entire time I am lying as he put it on me. I know psychology works and it worked on him. Anthony went faster. Each time he felt his nut coming, I would lock my pussy on his dick head like the queen I am, so as he pulls out, he could feel my pussy grip on him. Anthony is no different from other men. My body did this move, he could not take it. No warning prepared me as Anthony took his long dick out my pussy and inserted it effectively into my asshole. I shouted to the top of my lungs. I didn't count on anal sex, but this is what he likes and for a short spell, so will I.

People do not understand that if you are the outside woman, it means taking dick however and whenever he likes it. For him to go pointless in me, says the wife doesn't let him. That idea made my ass wetter than my pussy. Anthony grunted and grinded on me with all his strength and I did not know if I could take it. Each time he pulled his huge dick out, I know my guts came with him; this is how strong and dynamic he's taking me. I could only pry my nails into my clammy thighs as he rode me faster. My words could not come out my mouth.

My brain wasn't thinking. It could not think.

Anthony terrorized the asshole and marking his territory. My man made known no other man will ever do this to me but him. For the most part, he is right. I didn't reach an orgasm and didn't care. He has stunned me, and my body is in a sexual shock. Anthony said, "Here it comes."

I heard those words of joy. My lover charged the pussy like a runner with the finish line in sight. A moment passed and he, raining wet with sweat, stared at me. I didn't say a word as he eased the huge dick out my ass. He lay beside me. I let my trembling legs fall to the bed as he told me, "I've never experienced sex like this before, with no one. And I mean no one. Yours is the best and I don't want anyone else getting my pussy but me. Is that clear?"

"It's clear if you my man."

"I am now, and we will be going to church."

"I like your church," I added with feelings that our relationship was now God approved, since he brought up church right after our sinful act.

"Okay, we will go there."

He leaned up and kissed my lips, nothing like a friend. He touched my stomach. "I wish I could put a baby in you."

"I wish you could too."

I became silent as I said from within,

"Anthony, I will always be here for you, and you will always have a part of my heart."

"I know what you have faced. I know your heart and I know you really love me. I also know you are wife material and let no one tell you any different."

He got up and showered. I must make him see I am all he needs and not her. I picked up his unlocked phone and went through it. She did call and text him. He's not lying. The water turned off. I put the phone down and lay on the bed. My man said, "Where are the boys?"

"They at my sister's house, for now."

"Let's go get them so we can go to the zoo."

I gave him a joyful smile of happiness, and know the boys will be equally joyful. This means being seen in public with us and not her. I asked, "You sure? I mean, this is public."

"I am. I thought about it as I showered. She left me, like you said. It's her loss and what I do or don't do while we are separated is my business. I still have to live my life and how I choose is up to me. I guarantee it won't be lonely."

"You got me?" I added.

"And, Ley, I got you. You don't have to worry about anything or anyone."

"Okay. I believe you, Anthony."

I put on a short off the shoulder dress, with no panties or bra. My breasts are perky and my ass is round; yes, I have a body worth dying for. The way he looks at me and smiles, gives me chills. My lover placed his arms around me and said, "You feel good in my arms, Ley. I never thought of us being more than what we are. For some reason, I am glad. It's a new life for me, you, and the boys in it brings me joy."

"No Anthony. You bring me joy. I never thought I was lovable until you came in my life. You showed me things I never knew with spectacular mind-blowing sex."

"We better go before we end up back in bed," he laughed.

"I wouldn't mind. I can't get enough of

you."

I smiled and pretended to take off running. He came after me, grabbed me, picked me up and threw me on the bed. He straddled me as we laughed. My heart could not possibly take all these emotions he has given me. I lifted my head as Anthony kissed my lips lightly. He pulled back, to taunt me. I like this challenge he is giving me I thought, as Anthony spoke, "Let's go."

We got up and left in his car. I am not nervous I thought. Anthony gave me courage to forget about him being married. We drove to Paisley's house. She saw me get out of the car. My sister waved at Anthony and asked as we walked inside, "You all out in public?"

"She done left him and last night we made magical love," I spoke with such a glow.

"He your man now?" my sister asked in a strange way.

"He says he is why he wouldn't?"

"You threw the pussy on him like that, after months of chasing him?"

"It's worth it. I mean, I would tell him I'm sorry for causing problems in his marriage. Truth was I wasn't really sorry. I mean, I wanted him to myself, and he is just as much to blame as I am. I wanted to meet his wife but after he and I became closer he told me no. Hadley became jealous and didn't want us talking. You remember how insane and depressed I became when he left me alone?"

"I remember and can't forget. It took a while for you to snap out of it and he hadn't slept with you then."

"I know, Paisley, we weren't having sex like that. But after last night, I can't and won't lose him. The way he made love to me and told me he doesn't want anyone else getting it, spoke to my heart. I don't care about her being his wife. She left him and I plan to be all he needs. But you know what?"

"What?"

"If she hadn't called talking shit, I wouldn't be with him right now. I told her dumb ass I lost all respect for her. A part of me wanted to let him go because he is married. But he found me! Don't the

Word say something like, 'A man who finds a wife;
he finds a good thing and favor.'"

"Yeah, but you not his wife and if you were
his wife, would you want him talking to a woman
like you?"

"What you mean?"

"Would you want your husband talking to
another woman on the phone all the time; one you
think may have evil intentions?"

"Hell no. He won't need another pussy to talk
to but me."

"But you think it is ok for you to do it?" she
stated

"I wouldn't do it if he didn't say so. He has to
check me, not her. He kept talking to me and I kept
responding to him. She is his problem, not mine."

"When you became a part of their marriage,
you became their problem, not hers. Twin, don't
you have morals? Don't you know men lie, just to
get what they want? He's lying to her and he's lying
to you. He's not faithful to either one of you, and
you deserve so much more than he has to offer. I

don't want you to be second to no woman."

"Have you ever loved a man like Anthony?"

"No. I've never loved a married man before." she spoke.

"Then you can't imagine the love I have for him and him for me. I used to think no man would want me, but he does. My harsh past does not hurt who I am in his eyes. I didn't think I had anything any man would want. Meeting the love of my life changed my life. Anthony even says I am wife material. Sounds crazy, Paisley, to have morals and believe all this man says, but I do. He has me sprung on who he is, more than what he does."

"Well, it does sound crazy because he is married. Twin, I won't lie to you."

"I guess you on her side?" I questioned her loyalty.

"I am on the truth's side. The truth is may be twins, but we don't think or act alike."

"I know but he isn't happy with her. He would tell me how she isn't doing what she needs to, and she is never there for him or understands him. He has told me how he didn't love her when he married her. In fact, he said he learned to love her, but he's not in love with her."

"Yeah, but Twin, if he's not happy or in love with her, why can't or won't he leave her? She can't be that bad. Besides, he can't make decisions about his marriage with her if you cause problems, on purpose or not. Stay out of it. Let them legally separate or divorce. When that happens, go full force. Until then, she is still his wife and if she comes back, what happens to you? You are better than this."

"Yeah, but Anthony makes me happy and naughty. I have never felt this way about a man until now. I didn't start out trying to break up his home. She did that. I was just being there for him, like he been there for me. I mean I hate he is going through this but what about me? Her loss is my gain. Can't I be happy for once with the man I love and who also loves me?"

"Twin, how happy do you think you can be with another woman's husband? You can't build your foundation off her tears. Who knows what all she been dealing with, when it comes to him? God will punish you and him for what you are doing to his wife. I don't care if they are separated and have been for years. They are still legally married and you, my dear, are having an affair."

"It's not like I hadn't had a church man before."

"That was then. You are different now, remember? You changed your life and doing better, if not for you, for the boys."

"I know, but what I also know is, right now he is mine. I plan to make love to him and make him see he needs me and not her. Anthony is going to know who is there for him, like me. I plan to ride this out for however long. I love him and don't want anyone but him. His wife can go to Hell."

"The things you say about her could be about you," my twin stated.

"It's not that. He and I started off as friends, but he showed me how good of a man he is, and I fell for him; hook, line and sinker."

"You forgot his wife fell for it too. We don't

really know what goes on in their home. There's a reason why he is with her and hasn't divorced her. Use your head, not your legs Ainsley."

"She is not like me. She doesn't deserve him and if he didn't want me, he would leave me alone, but he didn't. He hasn't. He tried, but he still comes back."

"Twin, I don't have a good feeling about this."

"Why would you? You had a handpicked life. You weren't raped by our uncle for years. You never had abortions or participated in threesomes. You were never used by men or yearned for real love. You had it made, and I didn't."

She was quiet before she said, "I may not have suffered, but you make your own choices now to do right. Your past can either make you better or bitter. You can't change the past, but you can start now, by making better decisions. He's married, leave him alone. If he's in a relationship, leave him alone. You don't know the mindset of the other woman. You don't know what she thinks. You only know what he tells you and that could be lies. I don't see a future for you and him. You have two adorable sons, who don't need your bad decisions following them. Believe it or not, what you choose indirectly affects your sons. Just think about what you are really doing."

I was quiet. She knew she told the truth, but hurt my feelings. Taking a sigh, Paisley spoke, "Ley, I see your mind is made up about this situation ship. I just hope you are satisfied with your decision."

I laughed at her unfamiliar word for my situation. I smiled with joy while saying, "Be happy for me and wish me the best. I need it right now." Paisley gave me a fake smile as she didn't answer. I waited. She avoided my statement as she said, "Your boys are around back."

We walk outside towards the bench. The boys were out back playing with Anthony. He was teaching Jared, my four-year-old, how to swing a bat. I felt so much joy seeing my boys happy and thriving. He finished with Jared, and then he showed my two-year-old son Kyle how to throw a football. They were watching him and learning. A complete turn on, I thought as I felt warm all over. They saw me and paid me no mind. I liked that. Paisley noticed my expressions and spoke quietly, "I hope you are happy and if I could, I would help you."

A light went off in my head. "There is something you can do for me." We sat on the bench, and I said, "Carry a baby for Anthony and me."

"What?"

The look on her face was beyond priceless. She could barely close her mouth. I laughed and she said, "Repeat that, because I don't think I heard you right."

I repeated it with much enthusiasm. "I want you to carry a baby for me and Anthony. I don't have a uterus and you do. Paisley, you are my twin, and we have the same DNA genetic make-up. You know I would do it for you if you ever needed me."

"Does he know you asking me to do this bizarre thing?"

"He doesn't. The plan just came to me. I'll

make him use a condom and go from there."

"Are you serious?" I heard in a surprise way.

"I am. He told me he wishes he could get me pregnant and so do I."

"Ainsley, he could have been talking out of his head in the heat of the moment. You talked about the Word a few minutes ago. Now it's my turn to tell you. The Word says, 'Neither be partaker of other men's sins.' I don't want to be in on what you are trying to do. I could get in trouble or be in the middle of the mess y'all doing. Worst case scenario, his wife could blame me for shit you caused. I can't have that."

"At least think about it. I would do it for you if you asked and you know it."

Before she could answer, Jared came over saying, "We ready."

I gave my sister a hug and we got in the car. Jared buckled his brother down as Anthony drove. The air is blowing, and I felt happy. The boys were quiet, and my man is driving his new family. That was short-lived until Hadley called. Anthony looked at her calling and didn't answer. He said, "When I am with you, I don't need her calling."

I didn't say a word, but inside, I was relieved. We kept going and finally we arrived. After we got situated, Anthony spent all his time with them. I wasn't mad or anything, I am glad he is there for them. All day we took pictures, ate and carried on. This man is being the most perfect man. I could tell he is enjoying himself with us. You can't help but love him. Too bad he is married, but I won't think on that. He is with me and there is no wife. She doesn't exist, I thought as stared at him.

Throughout the day, each touch from Anthony invited thoughts for the night and he knew it. It is the look upon his face as his hand touches mine. He knows what he is doing, I thought as I arched my breast. I think he is getting this pussy again tonight and this time, I'm sucking dick. As if he read what is on my mind, he didn't say a word then. We got in his car and locked the boys down. I purposely opened my legs. My man turned the ignition on. He didn't drive off as we sat there in the parking lot.

He fixed his eyes on me and stated in a tempting way, "I know what you thinking."

"You do?"

"Yeah, I do."

"You know me that well, as to read my thoughts now?"

"I know you well enough, Ley."

"Then tell me, what am I thinking?"

"How about I let you show me, what you are thinking?"

He looked over his shoulder at my boys. They were about sleep. He deliberately threw his hands on my left knee. Gazing in my face, his masculine hand glided up my thigh. I am caught off guard again by his seductive behavior. Anthony didn't stop. Those fingers of his flickered my hidden bald pussy as he said, "I may be too weak to go home."

I made a panting sound as he did that. I assumed he'd stop but his fingers inserted themselves into my dripping wet vagina. He used his left hand and began driving. While the boys were in the back, I leaned my back to meet his hungry fingers. I can't believe this is happening. I can't believe he is heating me up and it's dusk-dark, I thought. My lover is full of surprises. He is making me horny and thirsty for him with my children around. I cocked my head to the right to gasp, trying to keep from shouting out a window. Anthony spoke, "No matter where you at, if I come, you will cum."

My breath became hollow like an empty rotten log. I wanted to scream and jump up and down on the whole hand. I wanted to grind them into the seat, because no set of fingers had ever brought on such liking. I felt the orgasm coming strong like a storm brewing. Before the completion and the body jerking, Anthony removed his fingers and planted them in my mouth. I closed my eyes. In my mind, it was his dick. I sucked my own juices, and I caught a dry nut as his fingers slid out my mouth.

I noticed we were at his house. It didn't look like the same house I had seen. It's smaller, but comfy. I asked, "Why are we at your house?"

"I want you to see how serious I am about us now. I don't have her, but I must go on. She made up her mind to leave, so fuck it."

"Yeah, but why at her house? She could come back at any time."

"She won't come here. Do you trust me?"

"Yes. I trust you with my life."

"Okay. Let me handle Hadley. She is nothing for you to worry about. She is my problem and not yours. I got you."

"You got me?"

"Yes. I got you. Let's bring the boys in."

We unhook the seatbelts and he went in first. To begin with, the house looks like it's barely used. Then again, they don't have kids, and no one is there to mess anything up. It wasn't too crowded but just right. I followed him as we took the boys to a medium bedroom with a full-size bed. We undressed the boys and covered them up. I left the door ajar as I followed behind him. Anthony took me back to the open space. Once he turned on all the lights, I saw a huge and spacious living and kitchen area.

I really like this small house already. He said, "Follow me."

He took me to the room, and I saw a bed big enough for a king's round table. I never saw a bed so huge. He asked, "You like it?"

"Anthony, this house is really nice."

"It's a lonely house, but not anymore. I plan to have you and the boys with me a lot."

"I don't mind, but this doesn't look like the house I had seen."

"It is a part of it. The rest of the house is beyond the fence for privacy."

"I don't understand."

"Hadley left this for me to do what I want. I can have who I want back here."

He saw my uneasiness. My lover placed his hands around my hips and persuaded me closer with his smile and charm. Using his warmth and touch, I am like crushed ice in a summer's sun. This faithful friend of mine has me under his spell and it makes me scared for a man to have so much control over me. He brushed my hair back for a tender kiss on my lips. I closed my eyes for emphasis. I opened my eyes and saw the most loving face ever. This gentleman said, "I've been waiting to kiss your lips all day."

"What else you waiting to kiss that I have?"

He smiled and said, "Let me show you out back."

He opened the French doors in the living room; I saw a huge in-ground pool. It had patio furniture, a bar, a sand pit on the side, with swings for children and the nicest outdoor kitchen ever known. *This house must be for entertainment,* I thought.

Speaking softly, "Seems like you only entertained company here."

"We did. You must remember, we don't have children and we don't have anything else to do but entertain her clients and guests. She always has big parties with a lot of important people here, like policemen to judges, from lawyers and DA's and from people in Washington D. C. She has a lot of pulls and her Gorgas family is well-known."

"What about you? What do you entertain?"

"I entertain a woman who has time for me. She and I laugh, and we have fun. She listens and she gives me her opinion, but I don't mind. This woman also has boys I admire showing manly Godly things."

"What you want right now for entertainment?"

He took off his clothes in front of me. I saw up close how hung he really is. I could not take my eyes off such a marvelous pleaser piece. Making his fingers snap, my head jerked up. Those hands, that body has my attention. Anthony said, "I take it you love it."

I walked over to him and touched his manhood. The way it became heavy in my hands amused me. Anthony let me stroke him and before I could do more, he touched the edge of my dress and pulled it over my head. My dress rested in his hand as he stared at my huge breasts. I held his gaze and spoke, "You like it?"

"I love them. I can't keep my eyes off them. They fit just for me and only me, Ley."

Anthony threw my dress on the ground and put me in his arms. I could get used to this, I thought as I wrapped my arms around him. He started walking. I didn't ask where he was going, and it didn't matter. I would follow him through a fire. The next thing I knew, he jumped in the pool with me in tow. I screamed as my body splashed in the freezing water. He laughed at me, and I laughed too once the shock wore off. Anthony let me go and we stood in four feet of water, face-to-face for a moment. My hair is soaked, and my love kept staring at me. I felt uncomfortable.

He didn't say a word. He only looked at me intently. "I wish I had met you before I met Hadley. My life would be different now. I would be happier, and I would be with a woman who is there for me."

"I wish we had met too and all the things I've gone through may not have occurred."

"Life has a funny way of getting our attention. I would still be miserable and wondering if there is more to life than working on my little job and being a showoff for her at parties."

"Anthony, I can't make up for the sorry life you had with her but from this point on, I can be the woman you need right now. I know we can have something special if you want it. I know I do. You are the man I have been dreaming of my whole life. You are more than just Anthony; you are my Anthony and it's personal. You see me for who I am and what I use to be. You don't let my past scare you and you love me. I could not ask for anything better in life than what I have right now."

"I thought the same thing, when I first noticed my feelings for you."

"You did?" I asked.

"Yes. She accused me of you so much, that

she saw how I felt before I did. I didn't want to hurt her, but how could I not? She has everything and you have nothing. My days are no longer the same, since I met you. I no longer look at life as plain. You keep my attention and allow me to be the man I am, while she did everything and allowed me to do nothing. You hold me accountable when I try to ignore my feelings. With Hadley, all I have to do is get mad and she quits talking. We grew apart, because I was living her life her way and I was miserable, long before you. This day, I can truly say, being in your life is the best decision I have ever made."

"Anthony, hearing you saying that means a lot to me."

"Shush. No more talking. I need to feel you."

He carried me closer towards the edge. I placed my hands flat on the tile surroundings the pool. My nipples were standing at full attention as the perky things bounced in his face. Anthony said passionately, "You are very beautiful, and I can see why women think you are a temptress."

I moved some and so did my breasts. The sight of them made him anxious to be in me, because he lifted my motionless body up to meet his. My legs found his waistline as he pulled me closer and held me by my waist. I promise, this time when he entered me, I felt love and undying affection. I didn't want to move and really couldn't. Anthony is pumping me slowly and with feelings. He was making me go through the changes of slow fucking. The waves of the water didn't make it better. He's already wet but this time, he had his eyes fixed on me as he moved and swayed with the small currents.

The love of my life is doing unusual things to me. I continued taking the intense beating from him and the pool's edge. My man is giving me something I can touch and it's wonderful. Nothing could stop what we are doing. We went from talking to fucking in a matter of months. If I had known he would be this easy and this caring, I would have made my move sooner. However, it took me tricking him into feeling sorry for me, and her leaving him, for he and I to be where we are now in our lives, I thought as he brought my thoughts back to him with the words, "Put some nut on my dick."

I'm not as amped up as he is, but hearing his commands, made my body react. I saw how intense he was on making my orgasm rush, and I did like many women did; I faked it by saying, "Oh, yes! I'm about to nut!"

With years of practicing this technique I know how to sound believable. It doesn't take a genius to make your body shake or get wetter. On the other hand, he didn't know if I were real or not about the orgasm. He was digging off in me deep and hard, while pinning me to the edge of the pool. My man was reaching his peak and making sure I felt all his crushing authority on me. Anthony kept pushing himself in me harder and harder. He was stepping on his tiptoes and rising backwards. He was making his dick pull me to him.

My thoughts left me thinking, he is torturing me with a good fuck. You can't get mad at your man for putting it on you good or claiming your body that's his only. He is trying to compete with no one. For now, I will let him think there could be others because of the roughness. Oddly enough, married men have given me the best sex in my life. They know how to make a woman like me feel good. They take out any anger they are expressing on my lower parts and in the process, they fall in love or can't leave me alone.

I don't know what he is trying to find but he won't find it like this. He will end up craving me and not letting me go. Then again, I would not change the way he is giving me the business. He is making it damn good was overwhelmingly special. I needed this pussy to be better than his wife's and to be convincing I made those small little jerks after his big release. Those jerks make my pussy grip tighter as it keeps his big dick inside of me a little bit longer. He moved some, but I did not let my legs fall. Anthony got the hint and propped his head into my breasts and kissed the valley.

He rose up. "You're too much for me and I know your orgasm was weak but hold on. Let me get out you this water."

He elevated my body on the edge and sat me on it. He is still eye level to the breast he claims to enjoy. He said, "You don't think you are special?"

"Honestly. I do and I don't."

"Why is that?"

"I know I mean something to you, but you say its love. I am not sure because you love you know who."

"Really?"

"Yes. I mean, we've spent a lot of time talking, but made it official last night. I am more than a booty call or a good time girl. I need stability, and sooner or later, commitment. We both know I can be the perfect wife, given the right elements. But I have boys who need a father figure, not just a mere boyfriend here and there that interrupts our lives at will."

"You know, Ley, how I always talked about not hurting her but here I am following behind you, like you and I only exist. I can be the father figure they see and those months away from you all hurt me just as much. You don't know the half of the shit I went through without you. I couldn't talk to you, and then it hit me. I am a grown ass man who enjoys the company of a woman who makes me feel important. This woman in my presence encourages me, gives me strength and comforts me without judging me. Ley, you don't tell me what I can and cannot do. You listen and we laugh a lot. But as for seriousness, you are my friend. I don't have that with anyone but you. I am risking my marriage just to have you in my life. Shouldn't that tell you something?"

"That doesn't mean anything, Anthony."

"Maybe not to you but being here in the house I once shared with my wife means something. She has been all I have known until you came."

"You telling me you never once cheated?"

"I've had friends she thought were lovers but was not. Right here, right now is what matters. I never thought I would be without her but it's you in the right now. That is all I care about it and want to talk about."

He lifted me up again and slid me back further. I thought he was going to get out and take me on the bare tiles, but he said, "You are becoming my world in this brief time. I thought about how much I love you all day today, and no one will ever take the place of what we have and what we are sharing. Oral sex is a special bond you share with the one you really love. Some people do it for a thrill, or for money, and it's wrong. This night I decree my unspoken love for you and I'm going to taste you with love. That is the difference."

No words were spoken as he parted my legs with his hand. Anthony rubbed the inside of my vagina in an up and down fashion. Those sensations crept throughout me. I kept waiting for his mouth, but I didn't feel it. His fingers were the only thing causing excitement. Anthony, said, "You have a very pretty pussy. It's so pink and I can smell how good it smells from here."

He used his hands and opened me up for the world to see. My man's mouth tugged at my pussy lips like a scared child. I nearly jumped off the edge and he hadn't done anything else to me. I did not see him, but I felt his breath as he deeply inhaled my natural pussy smell. He motioned his head all around quickly to rub my scent all over his mouth and nose. It drove me mad with want as my life partner began tongue kissing the very thing he touched.

A series of moans departed from my mouth to his ears. My spine is jumping out my back for him. My breasts reached for the stars on a stormy night, but none of that compared to the love I am feeling. He took his time with me, and any woman knows if a man takes his time with you, he loves you orally. There is no way he loved her like this, and she was acting up about damn phone calls between friends. Then again, she knows how skilled he is and how demanding his lovemaking is. I thought no more as his teeth gnawed on the sensitive parts of me.

I knew my boys were asleep and so to not wake them, I hollered loud enough for only him to hear, "Let me taste you! Anthony, let me taste you too!"

He did not respond as my body wiggled and squirmed on the tiles. Anthony locked his arms around my thighs. The tender flick of each tongue stroke drove me senseless. Nothing could break his grip on me as his face made a home between my legs. I kept murmuring, "I'm not ready to nut. Please stop. I don't want to nut."

My pleading only increased the madness. Orgasm after orgasm flooded me. This ripple effect was not gentle but rugged. The best part about it is how he sucked up all my pearly white secretions. I could not push him away if I wanted to. He kept drinking and slurping all I had in me. I assumed he had finished, but he mightily licked me even more. My spirit, man, shook with delight. He claimed the pussy as his own and I vowed he'd be the only one that does this. I closed my eyes from the mad flesh-loving appetite of my man who is feasting off me with care and proficiency.

Physically, I am drained from the two hours of lying on my back and feeding my man all the pussy he could eat. Anthony saw I was in a heavenly place as he pulled me back in the water. I could not stand. I rested upon him as he said, "I'm leaking. I need some more pussy."

"Fuck me any way you want my love, it's yours."

Regardless of how I'm feeling, if my man wants pussy, more pussy he gets. No questions asked and no request denied. This time he turned me around and allowed my head to sit on the edge. Again, I closed my eyes and waited for the infiltration of the love stick but it didn't happen. Anthony lifted me up and pushed my body hard on the tiles. My legs dangled in the water as I screamed, "Ouch! Anthony, that hurt."

"I'm sorry, Ley, but this won't hurt."

He patted my tan bottom and gave them a squeeze. I smiled because he is going to make it right. My man gave each cheek a peck and I am up to whatever. Anthony opened my anal passage up and with natural instincts, my asshole sucked in. The love of my life started blowing warm breaths in it. My only man inserted his horse tongue in the small hole. I gasped with excitement as my mouth fell open. A man has never eaten my ass before, and Anthony is being my first of many things. He used his tongue like a crayon to outline his artwork on each cheek. He tickled me as he went up and down the booty crack. I could tell he was engrossing my smell while his tongue went fast, then it went slow.

CHAPTER 4

Whoever said anal licking was bad and can never get wet has never had Anthony. This man has me going all over the place. I didn't know an anal orgasm could feel just as good as a vaginal orgasm, but it did. I was moaning and aroused by my own sound. My vagina was thumping as I felt my release coming. It was intense and powerful, more so than through my vagina. The sexual anticipation of climaxing from the rear was unbelievable. The voice inside me was shallow but clear as I called out for him.

Having a man please you totally is awesome, especially if he knows what he is doing. I caught my breath and Anthony laughed, while saying, "You never had your ass eaten before?"

"No. My God no" I spoke with honesty.

"I am the first and last, Ley. Come on. I want to hold you."

We got out of the water. Anthony and I headed to the bathroom to wash up. I went in behind him. He got in the bed first and was holding the cover upwards for me. He stated, "Come on, slowpoke. I am tired and ready for a good night's sleep."

I got in the bed, and he placed his arms around me. That moment in his arms felt so right. In my mind, I am his wife, and those boys were ours. During the night, we would switch up and I would rub his back and touch his muscles in a massaging manner. This bedroom scene has a normal feel for me and that lets me know, I am with the right man in the right place. But even if I wanted to, I could not keep my hands off him. These emotions are something I do not want to let go. I love Anthony and I know he has the same impression.

Until seven this morning, I was in my own heaven before my baby son Kyle woke up. He was crying and standing in our bedroom door. I put on Anthony's long shirt and went to my son. He was afraid. I comforted him and took him back to bed. I closed the door and made way towards the kitchen. I opened the fridge to see nothing there, just like I thought. What can I cook my family? I wondered as I looked and looked. Being the woman I am, I created a meal with bacon, flour pancakes, lightly sugared water and frozen peaches.

My mind was so caught up; I didn't hear my love come behind me. He wrapped his arms around me, and I screeched. He laughed and said, "Get your love right love."

Laughing was all I could do as he held me from this position. He turned me around and kissed my lips before speaking, "I hadn't had a breakfast cooked in so long. I almost thought I was dreaming as I smelled the food."

"You don't have to worry about eating. I plan to cook all the things you say you like. I love cooking and having a fun in the kitchen."

"I am glad you plan to do all these things for me. You have me ready for all the things I been waiting on."

"Sit down, sir, and get ready to enjoy what I cooked."

He continued to stand as he said while looking around, "You didn't cook much, Ley."

"You don't have much here for me to cook with."

"I know. I wasn't expecting you and the boys. It all just happened."

"Well, we need to make some type of groceries, if you plan on having us here from time to time," I stated while showing him the empty cabinets.

"We can do that later today."

"What you have planned?" I asked as I looked at him.

"I don't know. I have to readjust myself because I have boys to lead."

Hearing him refer my sons as his boys made my heart leap. Anthony spoke on. "You don't think I think of them as mine?"

"It's not that."

"What is it then?"

"You have been the only man who says that about them. Neither of their dads comes around. In fact, I'm just tired of the way my sons have been treated by their sperm donors."

"If you put them on child support they will comply."

"One of my son's dads won't stay in one spot long enough for them to serve him."

"I see."

"It's been an uphill battle. Jared's grandmother calls and checks on him, but she won't tell me anything about her son. He looks just like him and she says he has to be her grandson. The problem is the DNA test came back and I don't understand how my son isn't her son's child. His dad was the only one I was sleeping with. He doesn't want a retest and there's nothing more I can do."

"I am here for them now."

"I am glad. They need a real father figure in their lives. That is why it's so important for me to not have men going and coming in my life. They are young and very impressionable."

"Ley. Don't worry about what used to be. Focus on what is, and that is us in the right now."

"You have baggage to tie up. You know... Hadley."

"I got her. Don't fret about her."

"You all just split up and now you have me and my boys as your new family."

"If the truth is told, you all were my family long before she left me."

I was quiet as he said, "We won't talk about her. We are together. You hear me?"

"I hear you," I spoke softly.

Anthony gave me a squeeze. We looked around and the boys were coming out the room. He saw them and left me standing there. I fixed the plates and put them on the table. Anthony got the boys all settled at the table. Anthony grabbed my hand in front of them and they copied. I bowed my head and allowed Anthony to bless the food. I peeped and saw my boys copying Anthony. They were pretending to say grace like him. I wanted to cry. My sons mean the world to me and for them to have a man like the one I have in my life is everything to me.

We finished grace and the boys were eating. Anthony complimented me on how good the food was. I casually responded with love, but Jared said, "Yours are good. Momma's good."
Anthony laughed and I didn't get it. Then my son Kyle repeated, "Good food."

That was unusual, but I know it's because they are watching him. Anthony got up from the table and put his plate in the sink. My sons tried copying but they were short. I laughed and tried taking the plate. Jared wanted to cry. He kept saying, "I'm a big boy, Momma."

Anthony picked him up and let him put his plate in the sink. He picked up Kyle and did the same. I washed up the dishes while he had the boys playing horseback riding. They were having fun as I watched from a distance. This man is making my boys come out of their shell. Both of my sons listen to him and say, "Yes, sir." I have seen a change in them and it's a good one. One day, I will be Mrs. Anthony Vaughn and I can't wait. No more pretending and Hadley will be a thing in his past. I just hope Paisley thinks about carrying his baby for me. Why did I do a dumb thing by having my uterus taken out and my tubes tied? Those thoughts made me sad.

Anthony said, "Hold on a minute." They were wrestling each other. Anthony sat beside me "What's on your mind?" is what I heard.

Smiling at him, I did not say a word. He looked at me and I placed my head on his shoulder. "Out with it," I heard him say.

"You would think it is crazy."

"I've heard crazy before."

"I wish I could have your baby myself."

"I wish you could too. It would mean the world for me to have a son of my own. I mean, your boys are great, but there is nothing like a man's own son. That may sound crazy to you, and I would never mistreat the boys."

"It's not crazy, because I understand. I had been thinking of a way, but I know you may not agree. Never mind."

"Go on. I am listening."

Before I could tell him, Kyle was crying. Anthony got up and dealt with the issue. I was kind of glad. I wasn't sure if I should put it all on him at one time. We are now in a relationship, and I must be careful and tread lightly. He has been with his wife since high school, and I know he still loves her. All those feelings of love will diminish soon, and I am sure of it. Anthony said, "Let's take the boys out."

"Where are we going to go?"

"Don't know yet."

"I have to swing by the house and get their carry-around bags."

"I'll buy them new ones."

"Anthony. They have bags."

"But they don't have superhero bags."

I smiled because they don't. He told the boys he was taking them shopping. They were more excited than I was. He asked, "Is there anything you need?"

My first thought was for you to get divorced, and then marry me. Instead, I answered, "Your happiness is all I want for now."

He looked in my face and chuckled. "I read your mind and yes. One day you can be my wife."

We kissed. I spoke, "Let's go before we get caught up."

We went back and left with the boys. All

day long, we shopped for this and that. He bought fishing reels for us all. He also purchased a tent for backyard camping. This big kid seemed more excited than the boys. Jared got Superman while Kyle got a Spiderman book bag. Jared heard the cashier ask if he'd seen the movie; my son got excited. I already know what is going to happen next, but he didn't say anything. They called him Uncle and I didn't question it. In fact, I don't know what they should call him and don't know why they picked that name.

Our shopping trip kept on as usual. However, I did notice how Hadley never called him. I would check his phone and nothing from her. Once the phone rang and he said, "Go on and answer it."

"I don't know about all that. Your phone is your privacy, and I must learn to trust you."

"True... but answer it for my peace of mind."

The phone rang again. It was the automated teller confirming the doctor appointment he has coming up. He said, "We are together. I don't have any secrets from you. Any time you feel the urge to answer my phone, you do it. There is no other woman in my life but you."

"And Hadley," I added.

"She made her place clear the day she left me. She didn't want to be with me anymore. And its funny how being your friend broke up my marriage."

"Is that all I am? A friend?"

He gave me that boyish good look while ignoring my question. He spoke with a stimulating appetite, "You thirsty? I'm hungry and thirsty."

I didn't get it at first until he watched my lips and breast. I laughed. Anthony said, "You want to swap out? I'm sure you can fill me up."

Damn, why does he have to be such a damn turn on? I thought with a smile. My only response was, "I'll swap with you any day of the week."

He didn't say a word more. We gathered the boys and left. We went grocery shopping and grabbed personal care products. We were really acting like a family. Parts of me cried for joy because I realized how I am having my family, at the expense of him not having his family. It's sad, but it's all about me and my boys. They justifiably need a man to guide them. Their happiness is everything and seeing those smiling melts my heart. We will continue this life and be a family like other families. I can't allow Hadley, or my lack of not having more children, break this relationship up.

On our way back to my place, Anthony said, "I want you to pack a few things."

"Oh, where are we going?"

"I am taking you all to my main house."

My first thought was, don't go, but his look

persuaded me to. My second thought was what is the main house? So, I asked, "What is the main house?"

"It's the house I once shared with Hadley."

"You trying to get me killed by being in another woman's house!"

His laugh was jolly, but I was serious, and it showed on my face. I playfully hit him and spoke, "Don't laugh at me."

"Calm down. You talk about me trying to get you killed," he spoke with a smile.

"What I am I supposed to think? You want me in a house you lived in with your wife. That sounds like a killing to me, because that is what I would do to you and her, if it were me."

"We are separated, and she is in Alaska because her mom is sick. I hadn't heard from her and don't plan on hearing from her. She knows where I am at."

"Still, I don't know about that, Anthony. I have boys. I am not trying to get involved in whatever you both have going on."

Sounding sincere and caring, my love spoke. "I love the boys and I love you. I will not put any of you in harm's way. I am not stupid or dumb. If I didn't know what I was doing, I would not do it. The question is, whether you're going to trust me to lead you and the boys, or not?"

CHAPTER 5

He made a valid point. Since I am the black sheep of my family, I have done things on my own. I never had a man to lean on. No one has ever helped me and here I am, thinking about leaning on a man. My independence is on the edge of being gone. There is nothing more I love than to have a man on hand. Weighing all the impossibilities and what could be, I spoke from my soul to my love. "Anthony, I trust you with all my heart and if you say it's ok, then it's ok."

"Then let me show you how important you all are to me."

Going against my better thoughts, I said, "Ok. How long are we trying?"

"A few weeks."

"Are you serious?"

"Well, we can play it by ear, but we are grown, and we know what we want. We don't have to prolong anything. I refuse on being alone because she wants to. I will not stop living my life because she is dissatisfied with hers. I would tell her all the time, "You can't live my life and yours, worry about you."

"What does she say?"

"Nothing. Now her mom's sick, she has something else on her mind."

"You haven't heard from her?"

"Nope. Should I?"

"You used to tell me all the time how you love her and how y'all talk."

"I did love her, and we talk some but what I had with her is not the same for her."

"I see."

"See what?"

"You still love her," I stated while rolling my eyes in anger.

"Ley. I do love her. I have love for her. Hadley was there before you came along. She chose not to be here and that is her decision. I will not make her change her mind; although, I did at first."

"What happened?"

"Me being aware of my love for you is what happened."

I could not say another word. Moments later, we arrived at my place. I got out and gathered things while he stayed with the boys in the car. He has brought what it means to have a family to my life. I'd only heard about going camping, fishing and doing family-oriented things. If this is what family life means, then I want it by any means. I got back in the car as Anthony asked, "What you got planned for tonight?"

"Nothing, why?"

"I want to take the boys to see the movie. That's if you don't mind."

"I love seeing you spending time with them, and they love spending time with you too."

"So, it's ok for little ole me taking two very energized boys out to the movies?"

"I don't mind."

"Good, it'll be a boy's night out. I plan on spoiling them."

I laughed. If this is a dream, I don't want to ever wake up. If he has done this much quickly, I could only imagine what could be accomplished with more time. "Go on and have fun. Don't feed them too many sweets."

"I won't."

We made it to the main house. I was a little nervous, but Anthony made me confident and not cares if she showed up. I believe my love for he has not steered me wrong. I remained calm as he parked the car around back. We got out and went in through the small nook. Anthony took the boys off, as I admired the view. The kitchen alone was extravagant and poised. The table was neatly dressed and all the countertops, cabinets and exterior matched. It didn't look like children belonged here because of the single-person appearance. The house was one straight from a magazine, and it screamed elegant as well as expensive.

I hadn't seen a house like this since I left my parents' home. It's expensive and the rooms flowed. Nothing was out of place, and everything was perfect. Her taste is truly elegant, I thought as I kept looking. I didn't see or hear Anthony enter the room as he stated, "She had an interior decorator to put all this together. So don't think she did it on her own. Hadley isn't good at decorating."

"They did an excellent job," I spoke as I continued admiring the room.

"It doesn't have a true woman's touch."

"Yes, it does," I added.

"It is a touch of a professional woman, not a regular woman who decorates the house for her family."

"Yeah, it doesn't look like children live here at all."

"I am sure you can change it, can't you?"

"You want this house redecorated? For what?"

"I want things different. I want this house to look like a house for children. I want more than a house. I desire a home on this go-around."

That made my day. I smiled while saying, "Give me a little time. I don't want to take over or feel like I'm rushing."

"You aren't. I am starting my life over as a family man."

"You serious about us, aren't you?" I asked as he twirled me to face him.

"I told you I am. Get the boys. I need to show you all around, and then we have to go."

I got the boys and Anthony showed us the entire house. I was flabbergasted at the master bedroom. It was magnificent. The walk-in closet was huge and empty. Other than the house decorations, I saw no trace of Hadley Vaughn. He is telling me the truth, I thought as I loved the idea of her being out the picture. Some women would have a conscience about scheming to make the man you love fall for you. Most of the time it did bother me, but I deserve to be happy, and I deserve to have a family of my own. It's true, I don't want him sad over her; that's why I am going to replace her and make him no longer remember her.

It is going to take some time, but it will be done. I plan to let him lead me anywhere he wants. I will be his every thought and he will be my every thought. I must have zoned out as he asked, "You going to be okay, until we get back?"

"I will."

"You can go if you want."

"No, I don't want to intrude on you and the boys. Plus, I need some me time."

"Well, get them ready. We shouldn't be gone long, but if you need me, call me."

"Anthony!" I screamed.

"Huh? What is it, Ley?"

"You said if I need you to call you," I spoke with laughter.

He came over and kissed me. "Now go get the boys ready, while I get ready."

I went where my boys were. They were acting

happy, so I gave them a bath and they put on their superhero outfits. Anthony was already ready, and I loved the look he was reflecting. The boys were playing fighting. I said, "Alright, be good boys for Mommy."

"We will," they both said as my love led them out to his car.

Locking the doors, I headed towards the large bedroom. I saw a small picture of her and my man. She isn't ugly looking, I thought as I placed the picture downward. Next, I saw very long sex chains hanging from the ceiling, with handcuffs connected on the floor by some type of studs. They are positioned for the victim's limbs to be spread apart. Those must be for sexual play, but she doesn't look like the type who does those things, I thought as I walked in the bathroom. The tub was very round and huge. She must have had this specially ordered, I thought as I saw various kinds of bubble baths, bath beads and body oils. "This must be what it feels like to live like a queen in a castle," I loudly stated, while stripping off for the tub. Even the tub faucets have many water styles, jets, and temperature controls.

Turning on the water to warm and the jet streams to high powered, I soaked and soaked. As my eyes were closed, I thought I heard someone come in. My eyes popped open as my heart pumped loudly in my ears. What am I to do? I am in this woman's house, and she could come here at any time. What if she calls the police, saying I broke in? What if she becomes underhanded because I am sleeping with her husband? What if Anthony leaves me alone and goes back to her? Then what am I to do? My thoughts played with me about all the things that could happen. Suddenly, being in her home was a bad idea. My blood glucose started dropping as panic and fear set in.

I leaped out the water and let it out. I dried off quickly and put on my one-piece dress. My nerves were making me shake and quake, my head spun as if it was in motion. "Think, Ainsley. Think, Ainsley," I said out loud to myself.

Then I remembered the boys' bags. I picked up my bag and dirty clothes. Rushing downstairs, I went in my purse and checked my sugar. "It's too low," I spoke loudly as I put my glucose meter up and got my meds. My hands were trembling. I barely opened the bottle of Metformin. The meds were like candy in my mouth. Closing my eyes and retraining my thoughts about being in her house did not work. My sugar level is decreasing. I could feel myself passing out. My eyes opened and started searching for something.

My body led me towards the kitchen. I opened the fridge and saw orange juice, which I drank straight out the carton. I placed the container on the table as I sat down and closed my eyes again.

I allowed the sugary drink to rush my system. After waiting for ten minutes, it worked. I'm stressed and have every right to be, I thought as I went back for our things. A car pulled up and halted me. It must be her, my brain told me as I quivered like a leaf in the wind. I rushed in the kitchen and snatched up a razor-sharp knife. I went back in the living room and posted up behind the door. Soon as I heard steps, I looked to see Anthony walking in, and carrying my sleeping sons.

He saw my frantic, terrified look. Then his eyes dropped on the knife. Confused, he walked past me and put the boys to bed. I put the knife away. He came back to the living room and said, "Where do you think you going?"

"I thought all about it and I shouldn't be here."

He placed his arms around me in a comforting way. I sighed and he said, "Ley, I got you. You hear me? I won't let any harm come to you. Baby, you have to start believing in me more than you do. I am the one risking it all for you and the boys."

"I know, but you must understand where I am coming from. I am in her house, getting fucked by her husband, and loving him every day. What woman wouldn't act up?"

"I get it, but I won't let you get hurt. Remember, she left me and that opened the door for me to know how in love I am with you. She has been my world for as long as I can remember. It hurts, but what can I do about it?"

"Nothing" I spoke softly.

"It was her choice. We weren't doing it like that but now I'm tearing it all up."

I laughed as he said, "Baby, keep smiling. You don't know what it does to me. You brighten my day. We vibe and we have great chemistry. Our life conversations and you needing me is a blessing. You don't get that every day."

"I hear you. I'm just having my flesh act up."

"Well, tell your flesh it only acts up around me."

"Is that right?" I teased back.

"That's right. Now I want you to sit down and relax. We going to get this talk out the way and go on."

I went in the living room. What a grand room this is, I thought as I took off my shoes and placed my feet on the lounge couch. Anthony walked in, carrying two glasses of my favorite red wine. He's getting the mood right, I thought as he handed me one glass. My love lifted my feet and placed them in his lap as he sat down. With the glass in one hand, he used the other to massage them one by one. I closed my eyes as I drank on the wine. He said, "We will discuss Hadley and anything else, once and for all."

"I'm listening."

"She is a great girl, but her priorities are messed up."

"What you mean?"

"She is career-minded and not family-oriented. Hadley doesn't want any women talking to me. She has always run off any woman who comes close to me. She is afraid she will lose me, but her nagging me about you is what pushed me away. We got to a point of arguing over nothing."

"What was the nothing?"

"She would ask if I talked to you today. I would say yay and sometimes I say nay. Then you got to call a lot; mainly when we were together or in the middle of discussing something."

"I'm sorry about that and you know I am. I also don't know when she is around you," I stated in half-truth, because we women know when the main woman is with our man; we just don't care.

"I know, but she said she had a feeling you were up to no good. Hadley also claims you came after me just because I talked to you. Remember she called you a Jezebel?"

I laughed. "I remember. I was insane, beyond depressed, without talking to you. I was going through all kinds of changes."

"Well, change no more," he spoke as he sipped on his wine.

"Anthony, I knew then I loved you."

"I was feeling some type of way about you. I would argue with her just to go call you. It would be your voice I must hear. I would sneak off to see you by telling her I'm going out with the boys. She would call me out on loving you and tell me to go call you, then come back calm and talk to her."

"Was she right?"

"For the most."

"For the most?" I repeated.

"I could not admit my feelings for you while being with her. I would never tell her I didn't want her even when I knew I wanted you. I would take what we have to the grave before I let her know the truth."

"What about that affection thing?"

"She was right if she wanted to sue you about the affection, because you were taking all my attention from her. I alienated my wife by not being one hundred with her, because I was being the one hundred with you. The only thing she got wrong was us fucking. We weren't having a sexual affair then. Our affair was emotional and that is stronger. She left the door open for you."

"She wasn't a good wife, because she couldn't keep your attention. If she was a woman, she would know how to keep her lover interested. I saw the chains in the bedroom."

He laughed his sexual laugh. Anthony drank more wine and said with a firm tone, "No, Ley. Let

118

me get this straight. Hadley is a damn good wife and an awesome provide. The messed up part is I couldn't be bought. She would buy and or give me anything I ask for. All I had to do was ask her and it was mines. The problem is, she's what the word, territorial is?"

"That's the word she used with me" I said as I recalled my conversation with her.

"I won't say Hadley is this or that, because I won't lie on her. It was me not wanting her to dictate my life. She was grown and I didn't want to grow up. She was responsible while I wasn't. She couldn't keep my interest because I wasn't letting her. I wanted to run the yard and not be on her chain. I not being on her chain is what caused me to break away. With my wife, you must be ready and grown. There are no short cuts with her. If she gives you trust and love, she expects trust and love back. No more, no less. Her idea pattern is, if I can do it for you; you can do it for me. That is some of the reason why she acted the way she did about you and me just talking, because you are faithful, and I've given her reasons to not be faithful."

"Well, Anthony, I need a responsible man in my life and if you're not it—"

He stops me and says with admiration, "I am it."

"You just said you weren't responsible with your wife. You married her."

"I didn't have anything or anyone to be responsible for. I realized when I met you and the boys that I have to be more responsible. She has all that money can buy and then some. I didn't lack for much of anything, but I wanted a family. She wants to wait until she is further established with her career and putting more than a million back to live off on. She has always been the one in control of everything. All I had to do was roll with her flow."

"There's nothing wrong with that. I mean. What man doesn't want his woman to give him everything he asks for, if she can?"

"If a woman gives a man everything he asks for, she makes it too easy for him to leave."

"I guess" was all I could say.

He was motionless before saying more, "Hadley has money on top of money. There is nothing or anyone she can buy if she wants to. She has connections you wouldn't believe of and for most, which scares off many women because of the natural power Hadley possesses. She has rental houses, while I get paid a nice salary for up-keeping them. Hadley loves me with all she has, my wife just doesn't know how to listen."

"You only with me because I listen?" I had to ask.

"No. You need me, and I need you, while she doesn't need anyone."

"What makes you think I need you and she

doesn't?"

"Have you forgotten how you called in the middle of the night, and I always answered you, or how you were about to kill you and your boys?"

He brought back a memory I wish I could erase. Solemnly, I stated softly, "I remember."

"I was afraid if I didn't answer you, you would do something terrible, and I couldn't let that be on my conscience, wife or not. The hospital is for the sick and Hadley is not sick. I admit I have pushed her to a place she refuses to be. That could be why she has backed off. But trust me; she is a lion in waiting. She is waiting on a prey to get in her way, so she can make her move."

"She can be all she wants or think what she wants" I added.

"She never knew about your suicide attempt or the idea of murder. Hadley doesn't know anything really about you, unless she has you followed."

"She says you and her talk," I stated.

"We talk, but not about what she lets on. Your very name was an argument. She would accuse me of sleeping with you and I wasn't. She would tell me I was in love, but I would tell her I wasn't. Well, I believed I wasn't. Hadley would get mad because she would know it was you, I'd talk to all the time. I got to the point where I put your name under someone else's just to keep it hidden, but she found it and all hell broke loose."

"How did she do that?"

"She searched the phone records and began calling you, but you wouldn't answer the phone."

"I remember."

"My wife was pissed and hurt—"

I stopped him before he could say more by asking, "Do you have to say wife all the time? I know she is your wife, but you say it so much."

"I don't and I won't, but she is who she is. That's her title."

"For now" my voice said.

He gave me a devilish grin and stated, "Sounds like I hear a new Mrs. Vaughn?"

"Who knows? There were times I wish I were her, because she had you wrapped around her finger. Then I realized, I'm the one who has you," I stated back over the rim of my glass.

"Ainsley, it hurts me to hurt her and the pain I've caused her was unbearable. She kept staying with me, saying, 'She's here because she knows how she feels about me and Christ.'"

"Christ? What does Jesus have to do with all this? If he wanted your marriage to last, it would have. If HE didn't want me in your life, HE wouldn't have us to cross paths."

"Jesus honors marriages and we are married. I am only saying Christ has her and me together, but when feelings leave one, that one who loves less must put forth the effort even harder to make things work. I didn't do that. I saw us falling apart, when she didn't. She thought everything was Gucci when it wasn't. You do know the devil got in this relationship of ours."

"What does the devil have to do with this?"

"He caused us to have feelings we should not have had. If we kept it friendly, we would not be here right now. I believe she saw it because she tried warning me."

"You ignored her."

"She says if she stayed because of how she thought I felt about her, she would have been gone."

"So, she knew you guys were in trouble."

"I guess she thought our marriage became troubled when you came along."

"Why didn't you leave me alone, if your marriage meant so much?"

"That's a million-dollar question but for the answer I would say, need. She has it all together and you putting it together. She has high self-esteem, while you are relearning yours."

"Sounds like you need her and not me."

"Baby, I am with who I want. Trust me. If I wanted Hadley, all I got to do is call her and tell her I don't talk to you anymore, and she would come back. I am done with lying."

"Most men cheat for sex and if it wasn't about the sex; what was it?"

"Sex was never the problem. I don't want you angry, because your sex is damn good. But I can't stay where I am not needed."

I didn't like that one bit. It hurt my feelings to hear him speak of his wife, but I must know. He said, "I am honest with you because you deserve it. She is what I needed, but you are what I want and need. It was something about my attraction of you, from day one. I don't know if it's because you showed me how much you needed me, or how much she didn't need me. She didn't make me feel the way a man should feel about the woman he is with. She is financially stable and very independent. She doesn't need me; she wants me, and you can want a bacon egg biscuit even if it's not good for you."

He sipped on his wine some more as I finished mine. He got up and poured me some more. I said, "I am glad we are getting this conversation out of the way."

"Me too."

"You must believe me. I have done no wrong in your marriage. I am not wicked or anything as she says. I just know how a man should feel in a relationship. I saw how you were treated and knew I could do better for you."

CHAPTER 6

Anthony poured us some more wine and added ice cubes. He sat back down and replaced my feet in his lap. He was massaging my feet and relaxing me. The moment is perfect, as the mood increased. My love lifted my foot to his lips and nibbled lightly on my toes. I giggled and wiggled the toes teasingly. He put my toes one by one in his mouth; I inhaled in anticipation of what he is thinking.

"You like that?" he asked seductively.

"I do."

"I better stop so we can finish this and start on that." He gave my toes an individual sucking as he said, "Now let that linger as I speak."

I chuckled and stated, "We don't have much more talking, to do, do we?"

"Just a little."

"What about church? You haven't been talking about going, not like we used to."

"I plan to keep going to church."

"When?"

He didn't say anything. I kept waiting as he said, "We can start going as a couple when I let you know. Is that fine?"

"That's fine. Well, tell me this. You like me being here with you in the house she got?"

"Yes."

"It doesn't bother you I am here?"

"No. She left, and this is mine too. I didn't bring you here at first, because I didn't think you would be comfortable in here."

"I see, but know I am comfortable anywhere you are."

"What should we discuss?" he asked as he put the glass down and slid a little closer to my thigh.

"I want to discuss us and where we are going from here" I replied.

"We are here, and she is there. Let's leave her where she at," he spoke as his lips brushed my skin lightly.

"Anthony, please stop this. You are sugar to my blood and its rising fast."

"Ley, let me blow your mind with good loving," was all he said while he continued kissing my legs one by one. He lifted my leg higher. Anthony looked over at me as his lips placed numerous kisses on them. I put my wine glass on the table and pulled me to him without wasting his wine. He had my entire body close to his and upon him. He caressed me. Before we could continue, my son Kyle was standing there crying. Anthony looked at me. I said in a raspy tone, "Let me see what's going on with him. I'll be back."

I went over to my son and picked him up. He curled his little arms around my neck as I asked while taking him back to bed. "What's wrong?"

"The lady."

My heart jumped as I asked in a cracked voice, "What lady?"

"The lady who said we should leave."

Could it have been her I thought I heard in the house while I was in the tub? My mind questioned.

In hopes my son does not know reality, I asked in haste, "Were you dreaming?"

"Mommy, I want to go home," my son said.

"Son, were you dreaming?"

"No, she was standing over there."

"Where?" I asked as he pointed by the window.

"What she look like?" I asked to see if he would describe Hadley.

He shrugged his shoulders and I believed him. To comfort him, I spoke, "We will go home in a few. Lay down and I will be back."

He got out my arms as I searched the room. I didn't see any indications of anyone. My heart was everywhere as I looked and looked. In a hurry, my legs carried me to Anthony. He asked, "What's wrong?"

"My son said he saw a woman in their room."

"What woman?"

"I don't know, and he didn't say. I think we need to leave."

"Baby, let me check the house. You can walk with me."

I was unsure as he tried encouraging me. Anthony and I went all through the house, only to end up across the hall from the boys. The man in my view spoke, "No one is here."

"Yeah, but he saw something. I don't know what he saw, but my son don't lie."

"It couldn't be Hadley."

I still was not sure as I was still unsure. "Ley, come on. No one is here. We searched the house."

"I see, but it bothers me."

"Let me ease your mind."

"Can you do that?" I spoke without thinking about the good feeling I was just experiencing.

"That and much more."

I lifted my head back and laughed. Anthony used the opportunity of distraction. He lifted me up and I laughed while placing my arms around his neck. He carried me to another room. He said, "Door open."

The doors opened and it was another room. I looked at him and he said, "This is the smart room."

"Smart room?" I questioned.

"Shush." He muffled my voice as he said, "Tonight is your night."

"My night" I stated seductively.

He laid me on the bed and my thoughts wandered Has he ever made love to her in this room? Is he thinking of me or her? Why did he bring me in here tonight, after all this time?

"Clear your mind. Don't think about her, because I'm not thinking about her. Keep your mind on me and not have it all over the place."

"It was, but now you have my full attention."

"Let me help you keep it."

Anthony ravished my skin hurriedly with his mouth. I was calling out for him as he covered my mouth and muffled my cries. Doing what I needed, I pushed him off and got up. My love was speechless. Wearing my sexy smile, I pulled off my one-piece dress. His eyes watched the material fall. I looked down and slowly looked up. Our eyes locked, as lovers do. I have never made love to a man in his wife's house, let alone her bed, but she did leave him. Therefore, this is his house.

With that realization, I knew what I had to do. I needed to know if he loved me as much as he claimed. Purposely, I tested him on his words because his actions will tell me where I stand with him. I lifted one breast and placed the nipple in my mouth. My eyes were steadfast on him as he was watching me. Flicking my tongue, I lifted both breast nipples to my mouth. He is enjoying the show. And to be more believable, I released one breast to place my finger in my pussy. He smiled as I fingered myself. I took my fingers out my pussy and paused, the sexual temptation while piquing Anthony's curiosity. I slowly turned and walked out the door and a few paces down the hall. I heard him following me.

He is watching my ass; subsequently I touched my toes. Anthony walked up on me. His dick is a perfect match. He snatched my hips with his massive hands and bumped my ass just for me to feel how hard he is. Taking this fuck game a little further, I asked, "Don't you want to know where I am leading you?"

"No. Right about now, I will follow you all over this house."
I kept walking and stop at their once-bedroom. I was pressed hard against the door by his harden body. He moved my hair and sucked on my neck

from the back. This is too much, I thought. I didn't have to open the door. He did. When the door swung open, I saw a magical bed. It was huge and the kind you see in a princess movie. I fell in love with it as my body became ever so moist. Anthony said, "I can make love to you anywhere, especially in here. You are mine."

Walking into the room, I jumped on the bed. He closed the door and took off his clothes. It never gets old watching him undress, I thought. My man with his toned abs and muscles walked lustfully in my direction. He stood by the bed, his eyes begged me, and I obliged. Lying on my back, my head hung off the edge of the bed. He moved closer and faced me, straddled my neck while I opened my mouth. A few seconds later, my mouth was full of dick and nuts simultaneously. From this direction, his dick fit easily down my throat.

My lover's knees kept buckling as I pulled and tucked on him with all the affection I had. I thought the loving I'm trying to do in here, must be better than anything she has ever done. I don't care for him to fuck me tonight. In fact, it isn't about me tonight. It's about me fucking him in the one bed he may not want me in. He kept standing and as I kept taking the mouth torture, I must put it on him because I don't see any effect, so I pulled him harder into my bottomless hot throat.

His legs shook. I could not see his feet or his face. All I could see were nice sized balls and a nice stick to match. Yes, I am getting to him, I thought. Anthony's body shook as he tried stepping back. He almost got away, but I had a firmer mouth grip on him. I shall blow his mind and be the number-one woman in his life. There is no other way. I can't make up for all the time he was with her; however, I will make my head game the best. With that thought in mind, my sucking action became fierce and ruthless. This new sucking method got to him.

I was so absorbed in pleasing him that he stepped a few feet away. My mind did not rationalize what was going on. It did not have time. Quickly, the mighty man piece hit my lips. Anthony pushed himself in my mouth like a madman. He doesn't realize what he is doing to me. My eyes popped open. Seeing the joy he has with fucking my face by forcing his huge dick down my tiny throat. My love was grunting and grinding on me. He is taking over this love game. I could barely breathe. I was choking.

When you are in a panic state, your brain will send out gagging signals. My body was reacting to the message of vomiting. My backing up from the dick motion, didn't work. He kept on fucking my mouth with hunger. He wasn't letting up. I closed my eyes and went to a happy place. I tricked my mind into thinking all was well. I learned how to breathe through my nose and take dick down my mouth. The task was not easy, but I would not be outdone by his wife or his dick.

His speed was becoming rough, but I took it. This sex wasn't good anymore because I wasn't into it. I only wanted him to nut so he could stop. He is about to nut, I thought as I held onto his butt cheeks with all my might. I am not going to let him rough fuck me and get away with it. Suddenly, it happened. He froze and nut overflowed my mouth. I could not drink it all. He kept sighing like a relief was taken off him. He took a glance at me, and I slowly swallowed his thick white juice as he looked on.

My love smiled at me with approval. I, on the other hand, disapproved. I felt like a cheap whore and not like a woman pleasing her man. My thoughts were interrupted by him saying, "I never imagined how good your head game is until now. I'm very, very impressed, Ainsley Rudolph."

That changed my thoughts. I became kinky, using my hand to place the excess cum to my lips. He smiled again and got off my neck. For some strange reason, tears swelled in my eyes. Anthony came out of the bathroom and saw me still in the same place. I had not moved. He scooted me around and I sat up. He gave me a towel for my face. I looked up and said, "You don't think much of me, do you?"

"I think a lot about you."

"I'm talking about more than sex."

"I really do think a lot about you. It's just that we been doing naughty things I do like."

My voice gave a chuckle. Anthony asked, "Why you ask that?"

"You cum overflowed my mouth and you gave me a look."

"What look?"

"The look like I am a dirty bitch."

"What?" He spoke with laughter.

"I am serious that is how I felt."

"I gave you the look because I can't believe you and your techniques belong to me. No woman has ever made me feel this way. You know how to keep a man satisfied."

Those words made me feel better. He said, "Go brush your teeth and let's get some sleep. I need to feel you in my arms."

I went in the bathroom and noticed my bags were still downstairs. I went back in the room and Anthony was fast asleep. I made my way to my bags and went back upstairs. I made it to the top and saw someone go in my son's room. I stared and didn't see anything. I went in their room anyway and they were asleep. I closed the door back and went back towards the master bedroom. Closing the door, I brushed my teeth. Once I finished, I eased over to my sleeping man.

Without making a sound, I got in bed. His arms found my waist. I was happy, but still could not sleep. The longer I lay there, the more I just rambled in the mind, thinking how everything is going right for me, for once. I am in the presence of a man who found me when I was lost. He has been all I ever needed. He treats my sons like they're his sons and they adore him as much as I love him. Whatever I am in need for, he provides, just like a husband.

Then my thoughts pull down all the good feeling by stating, *he is not your husband. He belongs to Hadley and what you think he can do for you? He doesn't love you enough to divorce her or be seen with you. He is legally in a binding relationship; although, she left him. But do you really know why? Do you really want to know why she left, or do you want to keep believing the lies he tells you? What if his side is a lie? He does lie to his wife about you. What makes you so grand that he won't lie to you? He may be using you as a freebie and not taking you seriously. You did meet him while he was married to a woman who works all the time to support him and his lifestyle. You can't provide like that. Anthony could be playing both sides of the fence, just to see who would let him keeps playing. Better yet, what if Hadley is a victim like you?*

I desperately wanted to know, but he has told me his side. I won't dare call Hadley because she could tell me lies. I laid there awake. I sighed and just went to sleep, confused. The next morning was Sunday. I did not awaken Anthony as I got the boys ready. I went back in the room and put on a nice body dress for him. I didn't put on panties or a bra because the dress has breast pads. I loved the most recent look I have, and the better look my life has taken. I came out the bathroom and he sat up.

He stared and spoke, "I hope you put on a jacket or something. Those breasts are calling for a sucking."

I laughed and asked, "You like this?"

"So, will the preacher, the deacons, the mother board, the children—"

I cut him off by holding up my hand laughing.

"Which church you off to, Cinderella?"

"I thought maybe you could take us to a church of your liking."

He thought about it for and spoke, "I tell you what. You drive the Audi and I will be on."

"First, you don't know where I am going for you to be on later," I stated.

"I want you to go to my church," Anthony added with a smile.

"Your church, I mean you and Hadley's church?"

"You've been there a few times and she seldom goes. Half of the time she attends the church at the hospital she works at. Don't get me wrong, she loves God and believes I will change for some reason."

"Is it because she loves God?"

"Some of it, but mostly because she doesn't want a divorce and believes we can get through this "rough patch" she calls it. She believes if she hangs in here and prays things will get better. Anyway, we used to go there but now I seldom go. Besides the church is a public place to worship. Why? You don't want to go."

"I do. I don't want any problems."

"You don't have to worry about that. Didn't I tell you, I got you?"

"Yes, you have on more than one occasion."

"For once, believe me. That was her problem. She never allowed me to lead her as a man should his family. I am the head of the house and I make the final decisions on everything. Do you understand that, if I am to be your man?"

"You are my only man and I do understand. You have never steered me wrong and you have always done well by me."

"Good. Look on the dresser and get the

keys."

"What keys? Why aren't you driving us?"

"You need some wheels to drive since you with me."

"I am driving the car."

"You are."

"Who car is it?"

"It was hers. She left it for me and I can do what I want with it."

I didn't like that. I pleaded in a pathetic way by saying sadly, "I really want you to drive us. This can be our new thing."

"I don't like the testimony service," he said dryly.

Laughter came out my mouth before I realized it. He smirked. "I am serious. We have a mother at the church that is long-winded. She gets up thanking God for the trees, birds, and everything. We have another one who gets sick everywhere and tells how God has healed her through her medicines. Boring."

I laughed harder as he said, "For real. She

doesn't know where or how to stop. It has gotten to where a lot of other people don't show up until the preaching starts or paying tithes."

"Fine, I will go on. You going to sit with us?"

"Aren't you my family now?"
I ran to him, and he held me as he lay back on the bed. "I know why I love you so much."

"Why is that, Ley?"

"You love me. You are full of surprises, and you understand me. No matter what happens to us, our bond is unbreakable, unmovable and unshakeable. The joy you have brought into my life is unquestionable. I'm so glad you found me as you did. My life has not been the same."

"Neither has mine. Neither has mine."

"I got up and took the keys. He asked, "You aren't nervous about driving her car, are you?"

"No. You got me and you gave me the keys; therefore, it's ok and she will be alright."

"That is the answer I am looking for."

With a zealous feeling, I got my boys, their bags and we left for service.

CHAPTER 7

The cocaine white Audi smells like a new car.
I have never driven anything as valuable as it
before. The feeling of being almost rich made me
feel some type of way. The interior was spick and
span. There weren't any fingerprints on the
windows. I don't think it's ever been on the road
before from the looks of it. I lock the boys down
and crank it up. I decided to take them to eat
breakfast. I didn't want to mess up the car, so we
got out and ate. The boys talked among themselves
as I admired them. I have seen a change in them
too, since Anthony's been a part of our lives.

He has brought on such a wonderful thing in
us. We finished eating and headed to his church, our
new church. The last line stating, "our new church"
gave me a rush of excitement. Who would've
guessed, I would be madly in love with a man who
loves me just as much? I didn't but I am and I love
it. Since Anthony, smiling is a thing for me I
thought as I parked the car. I got the boys out and
said, "How do we act in church, Kyle?"

"Good."

"How do we act in church, Jared?"

"Good."

"Okay, we have that understanding. If you act up, you will get a spanking. Is that clear?"

"Yes, Ma'am," they both agreed.

The element of surprise hit me as my son, Jared gave me a hug. It was like him, but it felt somewhat odd. I gave him a hug back and said, "I love you both and you both are my world. I will give my life for you. You both hear me?"

"Yes, Ma'am," they both replied.

"Good, let's go on in the building and take a seat."

With me in the middle of my two boys, we walked to the steps. The doors opened and no one sitting in the pews turned to see who was walking in. I didn't feel uncomfortable, but I wasn't ready to sit up front. Even when I went just to see Anthony, I did not sit up front. Choosing this time, I sat at the back with my boys on the inside. A woman was testifying. She was rambling. This must be who he was talking about, I thought as I listened and listened and listened. She sat down, another one got up doing the exact same thing. Now I know why he said he waits until this part is over; although, this part is for the uplifting of those who may be going through it. *I hope they finish soon* I thought.

The more I listened, the more I tuned them out. I tried not to show my disapproval but couldn't help it. This church is a drag and I'm really trying to get into the service, but I can't. This woman caught my attention. She was whispering to another woman. They looked my way and for the most part, I read their lips. "How she feel showing up at his wife's church, pretending to be his wife? Shame on her."

I knew then it was my time to leave. I saw other people whispering, so I got my boys by the hand and stood up to leave, but the preacher said, "Don't leave." In haste, I sat my boys down with me. The others saw everyone looking, and they too grabbed a seat. The preacher spoke, "We come to service to hear what God has to say. Let us pray.

Give me strength to strengthen your people. Let them hear what they need and not what they want. We magnify you Lord, to lead and guide us to the real truth in Jesus' name, Amen."

I spoke, "Amen," and waited for the Word.

The preacher stated, "Open your bibles to Ecclesiastes chapter 1 verse 7. It reads as thus, 'All the rivers run into the sea; yet the sea is not full;' naturally just because it looks like you have enough, doesn't mean you have enough. You would think one has enough for what you can see, but when people have much, they crave more. This craving causes greed. They can never have enough money. They can never have enough power. They can never have enough of their earthly goods. They always seem to want more and when they do not listen to God on how to utilize what they have, they will use what they have for personal gain, Amen."

"Amen," the people murmured.

"The Word says in Matthew chapter 6 verse 19, 'Lay not up for yourselves treasures upon earth, where moth and rust doth corrupt, and where thieves break through and steal.' The Lord wants us to have good things, but everything we have is not good because of how we place our faith. If we being in human body and mind place our faith in what we can do, what can God do? If we believe we can do things according to our own accomplishments, how can it be God? If we believe we ourselves, make things happen because of who or what we know, why would we need God? Scripture in Matthew chapter 6 verse 24 states, 'No man can serve two masters; for either he will hate the one and love the other; or else he will hold to the one and despise the other. Ye cannot serve God and mammon.' Beware that learning about God will increase your knowledge of God. This knowledge of God will uncover the sin you have in God. Everything that is not of faith is a sin because faith changes lives as the Word becomes revived in you. Sadly enough, many people will enter to what is called vain less greed. Back in the scripture, 'All the sea run into the river; yet it is not full.' Imagine if you will a big body of water that keeps getting water, but never overflowing. You would think the water will cross over the water bank, but it doesn't. It continues to look full but deep down it is empty. Many don't know about being vain and or empty because they were brought up in a place where money, the looks, right connections, clothes etc was all you needed. This means everything, and they are steady trying to get more than what they have. To a degree that is fine, but what happens when you do that in God? What happens when you get greedy in God? I am not saying run to every prayer meeting, stay all day in church those things are good but is it what God requires of you. He knows your heart. HE knows you have good intentions to learn all you can about him. It is also true; you won't ever get enough of God because there is so much of God that one mere mind cannot handle him all. This doesn't mean you can't go to worship, just use wisdom. We could know about God today and every day we can discover something new in HIM and about HIM. If you are going to want more of anything in life, desire to know more of God, but use wisdom. You can't go to everything; you can't pray with everyone, and you can't neglect yourself. When you are tired, rest. God knows. God knows your heart and the very intentions you have. When you don't feel like going because you are always on the go, don't go. Every time you don't feel like going, doesn't mean it's the devil trying to hinder you. It could be God wanting you to rest, needing you to rest. What good are you to HIM if you are always on the go and not taking time out for your natural body to rest, so HE can feed you spiritually? HE needs you in a place for HIM to talk to you, but HE can't talk to you if you are always on the go, and never resting. If you want to be greedy, get greedy in God. As for being vain, allow the Lord to fill what you have empty."

I got up before anyone could see me. I got my boys in the car and sat there. She is right. I shouldn't be at this church, knowing his wife is a member here. I started the car and decided to take them to the park. The day shouldn't be a total bust. Jared asked, "Mommy, we not go back in church?"

"Mommy decided that we should have fun today."

The boys screamed. That brought me joy. I stopped by McDonald's and got them a happy meal. I wasn't hungry. The words of that woman bothered me. She was right but people act like I can't be happy too. I didn't make her leave; it was her choice. We arrived at the park. I had chosen a spot by the swings. I put their food on the cement bench, and they did not eat. They rushed to the swings, even Kyle with his small legs. I made them come back and eat. They didn't want to, but they ate fast. I cleaned up as they finished.

My eyes were focused on them swinging. I don't know what I would do if anything happened to them. Not thinking of anything, just watching them swing on the small children's swings with joy. I noticed this tall slender man out the corner of my eye. He had casual clothing and a smile. He nodded at me, and I turned my head but could feel him staring. From the corner of my eye, this stranger seemed to have something on his mind, because of the way he kept looking.

He was sitting with a woman, who seems to be ignoring him. An uncomfortable feeling set in. I was about to get up and leave but this time he smiled and came over. I didn't know what to think. But as he approached me, I saw the wrinkles and the old age. He asked, "May I ask you a question, ma'am?"

"Yes, sir, you may."

"If you died today, do you know if you are going to Heaven or Hell?"

He blew my mind. That is a question I did not expect. He stunned me. He asked again, "Will you go to Heaven or Hell if you die today; right now, at this very moment?"

With a whisper in my tone, my words were not loud as I stated, "I don't know, sir."

"May I sit with you for a moment?"

I nodded and he sat down where I could still see my boys. He said, "I was a minister back in my day. I retired after my wife died."

"I am sorry for your loss."

"No, don't be. She is with the Lord. I felt sorrow in my spirit for you and I knew the Lord Jesus would get me if I didn't speak to you."

"Okayyyy," I dragged out the word.

"Do you know what a femme fatale is?"

"No."

"According to Webster's Dictionary, a femme fatale is a woman who is very attractive and causes trouble or unhappiness for the men who become involved with her. She is a seductive woman who lures men into dangerous or compromising situations. She can either attract them by an aura of charm or a mystery."

I did not say a word because I don't know what this means for me. I had to question him further. "Is this what you think I am, a woman who lures men into compromising situations or whatever?"

"Ma'am, I can only tell what I see. It came to me to discuss sin to you and the course of its actions. I'm not saying that's what you are or was, but something is going on."

"Sin and its actions," I spoke unsurely, half-listening.

"Soon as sin is finished with you, you are no good. James chapter 1 verse 15 says, 'Then when lust hath conceived, it bringeth forth sin: and sin, when it is finished, bringeth forth death.' Once lust comes and you accept it, sin is welcomed in. You agree to whatever the sin is. You spiritually say, I like this wrong I am in, and you don't want to do the right thing. Soon as you have sin, it will take you far and keep you a long time. You can't escape death if you are outside of God in sin, because sin brings forth death and believe me; death is coming. Sin and death work together. It's a cause and an effect relationship. You won't get one thing without the other. The wrong idea is that people believe they can do wrong and have the good without a repercussion. God can't and won't bless mess. Young lady, people have lost the fear of God. They think what they do won't come back to haunt them. The world calls it karma, but God calls it reaping what you sow and sometimes, you fall, just to see who will lend you a helping hand. Sometimes that hand will help you and sometimes that hand will slap you."

"The man I am with now, was the hand that lifted me up when I was at a low point."

"But it's sad when you get off the route God has for you, just to see people for who they really are. Most of the time, that which you seek won't come from those you love, or those you have helped. People will lie to you and convince you how truthful they are. Believe me, they are the main snakes. These so-called loved ones will have you knee-deep in sin and up the creek without a paddle. You must listen to God for yourself and not let man get you in trouble. You have a brain; use it. Don't let anyone lead you in a ditch. You can do that on your own. Life has many leaning to friends' understanding and not to God's understanding. Sure, those you trust with your life can make lies sound good but that is just what it is; a sound."

"You saying if you don't be careful, you can get in trouble or lose your life; even if this man has never steered me wrong?"

"Don't be silly enough and follow man and not God. I'm making it known, sin will make you think it's a good thing just because the mood is right, or things are going well. Sin disguises itself in a man, woman, parent, job, material things, whatever or whoever. It doesn't matter who it uses to get you out of a place with God. The devil has attacked the Word of God to make you doubt living honest is not the best way. If the foundation is a mess, the house won't last. Doors won't close, one part is higher than the other, the ceiling will crack, the roof will leak and all kinds of other things. The enemy will catch you and wreck your foundation just to wreck your house. It is here you must know he is God. He can deliver you. Only he can truly provide for you. I know you want a father figure for your boys, and it seems like this man is the answer. He must not be if I'm telling you to be careful of him. Young lady, make sure the father figure for your sons is a true man of God. If he is a man of God, he will more than likely lead you the way a man leads his family. I don't know anything about you, but I know what I am led to tell you. Ma'am, hear what Jesus says. Follow your gut instinct and not your flesh."

"I love the man I am with, and he loves me. He has never done anything to hurt me or my boys. I don't appreciate the fact you are saying otherwise."

"I don't know why I'm about to say this to you, but keep in mind, the Lord won't bless you with another woman's husband; another woman's anything. HE has one in mind for you, and HE won't allow you to keep being a distraction in a marriage HE may be working in or through. If you are causing trouble and I'm not saying you are but back off; mainly if you know the wife disapproves of your relationship with her husband. The devil will have you saying, "We just friends or there is nothing going on." The truth of the matter is, she is still his wife and if you are intentionally or not keeping contact with him cut it off. If he calls you cut it off. The word says, 'Lay hands suddenly on no man; neither be partaker of other men's sins' keep thyself pure. Even if the man says you can call or he comes by to see you. You know for yourself it's not right. You have enough you must work on and being involved in what someone else is doing, will not help you one bit. The word says, 'Take heed that no man deceive you.' Get out of whatever the situation is before you can't. Understand you can't have what God has promised to another. Your husband is out there. The Lord may be pruning him so he can be the man you need and not the one you want. But you can't see the man who comes at you if you are involved with a married man who is involved with someone else. Be mindful and watchful. Again, I don't know you or your circumstance, but God does. I don't know your heart, but God does. Proverbs thirty and twenty says, 'Such is the way of an adulterous woman: she elated, and wipeth her mouth, and saith, I have done no wickedness.' Let me explain. Such is the way of an adulterous woman means, the woman is smart, can be very alluring and very conniving. This woman can be and most often is beautiful and enchanting. Her essence is so captivating that weak men fold in her presence. She eateth and wipeth her mouth means, she hides what she does. This woman is very secretive with her motives that are hid from all to see. Her actions appear innocent but her intentions are not; for those intentions rest in her heart. She only cares about what she can get and forget the rest. This adulterous woman could believe she deserves this or that. Whatever it is she wants, becomes her motive drives her, making her selfish and fleshly. I have done no wickedness means she pretends to be good but really isn't. She looks the part but denies all her wrong doings. The sin in her flesh won't let her own up to her ways. This woman will convince you that she is not guilty of what she is being accused of, but she is. I don't know what you are into but please be mindful. I believe you are a good girl caught up in the moment. Your boys need you. Do what is right and not what feels right."

He stood up and said, "I will leave you with

this scripture, 'He that has an ear let him hear what the Spirit saith unto the churches.' Enjoy the rest of you day."

I was stunned and dazed with no thought as the minister left. In a nutshell, he said I am a sneaky bitch who purposely broke up Anthony and Hadley. But it wasn't like that. She left him and he needed someone. Not just that, he has always been there for me, but it could have been anyone. I am not like what he says! I would never cause problems or harm to the man who has been there for me. His happiness means so much.

Looking at it from another angle as I thought, this man is right. I am driving this woman's car, sleeping with her husband and head over heels in love with him. I am in error and perhaps have the spirit of error following me. How could I have been so naïve and gullible for a man who wanted nothing more than friendship? Why did I have to sneakily desire him, which caused me in helping his marriage fall apart? I willingly sinned and somewhere in my heart I knew it. I allowed what I wanted to get in the way of what I needed. It's not his fault if I was needy, clingy and desperate. Anthony came in my life as someone I needed, and he became someone I couldn't let go. This man has meant more to me than anything and here I am eating, wiping my mouth and believing I have done nothing wrong, but I have. I really have! Having all this laid out in plain English made me cry.

I was weeping like a mother who has lost her child. I exclaimed loudly, "Lord I don't know what to do, right now."

Then I heard in my mind, doesn't Anthony make you feel safe? Doesn't he listen to you and has shown you how much you mean to him? I dried my eyes as I nodded my head yes to my thoughts. Well, quit crying. Tell him to divorce her or you will leave him alone; that way you are not wicked or an adulterous woman anymore. Problem solved. My thoughts were right. I gathered my boys. We got in the car, and I went straight to my sister's house. They love being at her place. She makes cookies and does a lot with them. She is more creative than I am. With this new event, I wouldn't feel guilty leaving them with her.

The boys were screaming and carrying on at their TT Paisley. They were equally excited. Making sure my face was clear, I explained how Anthony and I need to talk alone. She saw my urgency and gave me a hug. I so needed that. She got the boys' bags out and I drove off. I didn't know I had made it back until I saw the beautiful house. Anthony's car was still parked, and I didn't like the feeling. I got out and opened the door. I heard a crunch and looked down. There on the floor were red rose petals. I looked up and there was Anthony in the doorway of the dining room. He had a rose in his mouth with a smile.

"What are you doing?" I asked.

"I have a dinner date with my love."

"You do?"

"Yes, I do. Close the door and come on over."

I did as he asked. I could smell food and

my stomach growled. He saw me and said, "The boys not with you."

"No, they at my sister's house."

"I figured that."

He did not pay any attention to me or my sadness. I spoke first. "We need to talk."

"Indeed, we must. But for now, I have something to say."

"What's on your mind?"

"That is the same thing I want to discuss."

"Then we on the same page, then."

"All depends," I answered
"Before we get started talking about life, come on over and let me sit you at this fine table, fit for my queen."

You can't help but to love him. I gave him my sexy look as he pulled the chair out for me. I sat down and scooted closer towards the table. He sat opposite and said, "You haven't said anything about the table or the roses. What's on your mind?"

My eyes then took a gander at the table. Rose petals were spread on the table along with steak, potatoes, garden salad, butter rolls and white wine in elegant glasses. The table was beautifully laid. I gave my love a warm smile and said, "I'm sorry. I was so engrossed in my day that I didn't pay much attention. Forgive me."

"Ley, there is nothing to be forgiven. You want to go first, or shall I?"

"You go first."

He was talking as I started eating. "I didn't come to service because I wanted a way that demonstrates my appreciation of you. Ley, you have been a dear friend to me, and you make me feel like a man. You allow me to partake in the lives of your children and you let me show you love. This meal and night isn't about sex, although, I physically desire to eat you up."

Those last three words, "eat you up" practically made my pussy jump off my body and bounce around to land on his plate. The simple thought of him tasting me made me squirm a little. Anthony continued to speak. "I'm trying to show you that we aren't all about sex; no matter how damn good it is and no matter how much I want it right now. I want all of you and your character is one of the best things I like about you. We have fun and talk like real husbands and wives do. You want my opinion on things, and you do as I ask. You don't argue with me, and I've learned how to listen, for that thank you for letting me love you."

"I like that, Anthony, and I love you too."

"I know I am still married, but I promise you soon as I can, that will change. I want a future with you and the boys. I want us to live out the rest of our lives as husband and wife. I'm asking you to be patient with me. I am pleading you to hold on. Wait for me, Ley. I know we started out as friends, and I know you never tried to break up my home, but we were already having problems before you."

What the man said about an adulterous woman having sneaky intentions came to mind. I didn't have an ulterior motive, but one did develop. I bowed my head in shame. Anthony said, "Hold your head up. You will never look down. All those days are over. You hear me?"

"I do."

"I told Hadley I want a divorce and she asked me if I was seeing you. I told her it was not her business. She started yelling about how she endured me and the things she went through. I told her she didn't have to, but she insisted on being with me. She said she is hurting and can't think straight. I told her if she sends the papers over, I will sign them and give her all she asks for."

"What she say? What she do?"

"She hung up on me. I didn't call her back. I left it like it was. Now it's your turn to tell me about your day."

"I went to your church but left right after the preacher spoke."

"Why you leave for?"

"I didn't feel right."

"Was someone making you uncomfortable?"

"Not really, but one woman kept looking at me."

"Did you give her something to look at?"

"No. I should have," I stated with a

mischievous smile.

"What you do after that?"

"I took them to McDonald's and to the park."

"They had fun, didn't they?"

"Yes, they did."

"I wish you had called me, we could have made a family day out of it."

"I wasn't thinking. I was just being alone."

"What all happened?"

"A man came up to me."

I didn't say much more because Anthony kept looking strange about my saying a man came up to me. I smiled and halted his suspicion by saying, "He was an older man who used to be a minister."

"Oh, that really doesn't mean anything," he spoke kind of dryly before saying, "What did he say?"

"I was an adulterous woman who is sneaky and has intentions of being evil."

"Really?"

"Yes, but I don't believe it because I did nothing to break up your home."

"What else he say about you?"

"How I believe I have done no wrong in your marriage, and I need to get away from you before I can't leave."

"He too late," Anthony spoke with humor.

"Yes, he is. I can't leave you alone. Believe me, I tried."

"Do you believe you caused my marriage to fall apart?"

"Somewhat… I do."

"Well, you didn't and me doing this only confirms my love for you."

"May I make a statement?" I questioned as he ate some more food.

"Sure" he responded with a nod.

"If you want Hadley back, I will back off and let you and her make another go at it. So that way you can't say you would've went back home but didn't, because of me."

His mouth fell open and he stared at me like a child working a Rubik's Cube. My love sat back in his seat and scooted down, placing his arm over the back of the seat. I pray he doesn't see the position I am putting him in. Anthony is all I ever wanted since the day my life was supposed to end. He has been my all in all and that has never happened before. I just need a man to be there for me and me only. I know of his love for her, but I need that love for me and my boys

CHAPTER 8

I spoke those words in half-truth. I really didn't mean it but I must make him choose which one of us he wants. I won't have it on my conscious that I would not let him and her work things out. In my heart, I know my intentions were pure at first but along the way I fell for him and fell hard. I can't expect him or her to understand. They don't know what it is like to finally find the love you only been dreaming of; although, he is another woman's husband. Refocusing on Anthony, I could only feel joy.

His demeanor is unreadable but the hurt in his face is detectable. He looked up towards the ceiling and spoke, "If you mean it in your heart and you are truthful. Let me make love to you once more and then tomorrow we go from there."

My heart fell through the floor and bounced in Hell. He got up and came over to me. He turned me around in the chair and got on his knee. I had no idea a tear was running down my cheek. He stated, "I know you don't mean it, but you are right, although I know you mean well. I will call her in front of you when you want, so you may listen at our conversation. Please keep in mind, I am only doing it because of your request."

"Okay. I won't contact you and please don't contact me," I spoke with a lie beneath my breath. Anthony did not give me a warning as he ripped off my dress. I put on a show by letting the tears fall like a waterfall. Anthony pulled me out the seat and laid me on the dining room floor. I opened my legs and he continued to kneel before me, kissing my breast mightily. I moaned intensively in his ear. The more I carried on, the harder he tugged on my nipples. My arms wrapped around him and so did my legs. My lover was kissing me all over. I didn't want any interruptions, but he removed himself from my grasp and stated with deep breaths, "Tonight, there will be no penetrating sex."

I had no clue what he meant. Then he showed me what he meant by opening my legs and taking a deep sniff of my vagina. My breath was raspy with just the thought of him having his head there. The love of my life, licked on me in an innocent way at first. The more his head was there, the more the pussy flower budded out to him in a "take me manner." However, he paid no attention as he teased and taunted me with his massive pink tongue. I was bedazzled and out of my mind with want.

He needs to eat me up and take me out of my mind I thought as my legs flop over his shoulders and made a homemade grip about his neck. This lover of mine had nowhere to go as his head nestled deep into my hidden valley. I permitted him to get nothing but pussy in his face. But it didn't last. That loud orgasm had me hollering to the top of my lungs. It seemed like the more I hollered, the more he sucked on the clitoris with love everlasting. My legs trembled from the awesome feeling he was giving me. I've had my share, but none like this. No man had ever blown my mind by the intensity of oral sex.

If he was making sure no man came after him, he accomplished it with perfection. After the orgasm was over and my legs could not move, this craftsman continued with the mind lingering torture. My body was over-pleased and over-thrilled. The only thing left for me to do was cry. The tears kept falling and he kept sucking, licking and swallowing all I had in me. He has me hooked, now more than ever. This woman's husband has taken me over the top. My thoughts told me, you can't leave him or this alone. Let him think it is over and then show him what he is missing. That woman can't handle all of this. You are the better woman for him and soon enough, he will know it too. Soon as my legs fell from his shoulders, I glared into the man's eyes that'd just pleased me.

His entire face was moist from my secretions. He smiled and I realized a vow to not leave him at all. Anthony got up and said, "I am going to go get the boys, while you relax."

"Oh. I'm sucking that dick. I must have you put a cum mask on my face."

"No" he laughed. "I needed to get your scent all over me."

"And fucking me won't do that?"

"Ever since we been together, we been fucking. It's been damn good, Ley."

"You don't like it."

"Hell, yeah. I love the way you take all of me."

I know men can't resist seeing pussy and not fuck it. I opened my legs and he asked with surprise, "What you doing?"

I put one leg behind my head for a pillow. He lifted his head up towards the ceiling and laughed. "What, you don't like this position, or you can't handle this position?"

"Stay right there and find out."

Just like a man who has a weakness for sex and good pussy, I knew he could not stand to see a bad pussy waving at him in a mocking method and not do anything about it. He would go against what he said, all because I placed sex on his mind. He knows all too well how good and hot the pussy is. This sight of me throwing it visually sent a signal to his once soft pecker; now it needs to get a nut off.

The dick rises and throbs for a release. Right now, I am the only one in sight to give his cum the freedom it thinks he desperately needs. The willing participant took off his clothes fast and guided dick first into me. This collision made him shudder, then stop. I believed he was melting from our familiar union. He recovered instantly and began stroking me with all his power. This huge dick is in it to win it, not letting me go and that is exactly what I want. I don't want him to let me go. I don't care how much good pain I am experiencing from him. He needs to know I can and will handle any type of rough sex he gives.

The pussy rider closed his eyes as to make this a memory of our moment. My own mind saw the look and thought I too will make this a memory. I want it so memorable; he would remember the fucking we did in this dining room. I plan on ruining any precious moment they may have had. I will make him think of me all over this place and I know from this position; he will. But little did he know, this is "his only" pussy and he can get it any

173

time he wants. I just can't let him think he can. I will play hard to get and hard to keep. All games are put aside. My heart and love are on the line and I plan on winning the one I love, wife or not.

Bringing my thoughts under subjection was the sweat falling off his chest onto my face. My hair became soaked from the moisture in the atmosphere of sex. He was pushing his entire dick in me. Anthony rocked me and rolled me until I had another orgasm. My high was quickly met with his final pump of pleasure. His semen entered me like a warm introduction of heat to a cold room. I didn't want him to stop pounding me. I needed him hung in me longer, if possible, but that did not happen. The moment was over, and the dick was going limp. Anthony said, "You are truly a temptress I can't resist because I know how good the pussy is. The way you hold it there for me to get it all, drives me crazy. Too bad this must end for now, but I have a question."

"What's that?"

"Will you let me come get it at least once

a week?"

"You can't have your cake and eat it too," I sassed, knowing he can have it any time.

"I can have my cake and you know I'll eat it too."

If my pussy wasn't wet before, now it became super soaked. He slid off me and lay beside me on the floor. He said, "I'll get the boys in the morning. For now, let's go upstairs and rest."

Anthony helped me up and we went upstairs. I showered and he showered behind me. He came out while I was lying half awake and half hurt. There's no way this is the end of us, I thought as I waited for his long strong arms to touch me. He put his arms around me and pulled me near him. I swear I love this part of being in bed. I am not alone and the feeling of having someone in bed beside me at night is priceless.

During the night, I heard Anthony tell me, he went and got the boys from my sister. I ignored him and went back to sleep. Around 1:00 am, I awoke alone. I got up and went across the hall. The boys were in the bed asleep. I liked how Jared had his small bat in the bed with them. This boy loves baseball, I thought as I eased the door back and checked my phone. Where is Anthony? I wondered. I went downstairs and Anthony was still not there. I made my way to my sleeping area and lay back down. The rain was falling and making the weather good for lying up and cuddling.

Somehow I was asleep, but I heard, "You enchantress. You won't keep getting away from your evil doings."

I did not open my eyes fast enough before a pair of hands was all about my neck. I couldn't breathe. I kept trying to make out the face as the vision became clear. It was Hadley. Instantly, I was terrified as I fought back. She is a big woman who had little ole me pinned in her marital bed. Nothing I did got her off me. She was winning as I was dying. She said, "Bitch, you won't fuck in my bed again, with my husband!"

Suddenly I heard, "Get off my mommy!"

The sound "ting" rang loud and clear. I didn't

know what it was. The lights came on and it was Hadley, who fell on the floor. I gasped for breath. I sat up breathing hard to see my son Jared. Anthony had taught him how to swing the bat and he used it to hit Hadley. My son threw the bat down and ran to me hollering and crying. At that moment, I looked up at Anthony in the door. He had a petrified look on his face. He ran to Hadley's side and felt her pulse. She wasn't bleeding. This means she was only knocked out because my son did not break the skin. My love questioned in a hurry, "What the hell happened? What the fuck did you do?"

"I was in the bed, and I felt a pair of hands about my neck. I finally got vision when the lights came on to see it was Hadley. I tried getting her off me, but I couldn't. Jared hit her and she fell over. I sat up and I saw you at the door."

He lifted Hadley in his arms like a baby. He did not say another word as he cradled her. He picked her up and left out the room. I was a little jealous about the compassion he has for her. This man of mine appeared angry with me and my son.

He didn't think of her trying to kill me. Anthony only saw the effect and not the cause. Seeing I was not needed, I got my boys and their things. We went downstairs and she was lying on the couch, still out. Anthony did not pay my family any attention. His whole focus became his wife.

I escorted my sons to the kitchen. I headed towards Anthony and Hadley. He said, "I think you need to go."

"I already know my time here is up. Plus, I leave today anyway."

"Yeah, but fuck!"

"Why you mad? She was trying to kill me! If it hadn't been for my son knocking her out, I would be dead now! Don't you care about that?"

My heart broke some as he stated with doubt, "Just get the hell on. I can't think right now."

I didn't expect to hear that. I yelled, "You mad at the wrong one! My son saved my life and you angry because she got a knot on her lovely head. She will be alright! She tried killing me! You act like you don't care about me!"

He didn't say a word. I left him alone and called Paisley. She came over and Anthony didn't want to speak. That's odd, because he always speaks to her. I dismissed it. Paisley and I did not talk. She is my twin, and she knows I am hurting. I tried keeping my cool because I lost it in front of my sons. When we got to my apartment, Paisley said, "I will keep the boys. You need some time to think or whatever you need."

"Okay. Their clothes need washing."

"I'll do it. I will keep them for a few weeks. I will know when to bring them back to you."

"Okay," I spoke as I got my purse and my bag.

I got out and she drove off. I walked slowly towards my door. I could not function on all the events. Above all, I am surprised how angry he was about my son knocking her out. I could not rationalize how he acted as I opened my cold and lonely apartment door. For the first time, in a long time, I sat there and cried and cried. The sensation is not compared of anything I've experienced. The look on his face would not release me. The more I saw his facial expression, I ached more.

Physically, I was not prepared nor wanted to deal with the thoughts of Anthony and his actions between me and his lovely doctor wife. I was thinking, why was Anthony mad for no reason? Why was he on her side and not mine? Those two questions bothered me as I sat there with grief and pity. My life about Anthony had already consumed me. He must see Hadley was at fault, and not me and my son. Parts of me wanted to sell my soul just to make things right, but that is not right. I could not resist. I called him and he didn't answer at first. I called again and he answered with attitude, "What you want?"

"I was just checking on her."

"Why?"

"Anything important to you is important to me. I still love you as much as I did when I initially discovered it."

He was quiet. I was quiet. Finally, he said, "Don't call me back. I will get back in touch with you. I have to handle this situation."

Anthony hung up and I was left holding a dead phone. I lay on the couch and cried. If this what heartbreak feels like, I don't want it ever again as long as I live. The pain grips me and won't let me go. I know he is her husband, but it hurts as if he were mine. I didn't want to eat, think or breathe. Minutes turned into hours, and hours into days, and days into weeks. I know I can't keep pouting over him and must come to terms of leaving him for good.

Eight months flew by and I could not take it anymore. A new year was fast approaching and still, my love was with his wife. I got so tired of crying, it wasn't funny. Sometimes I would get a girlfriend to drive me by their house and I would see his car. I hoped to see him but I never did. I could not see his social media posts or anything concerning him. I was going crazy with myself and did not know what to do.

I even tried going to his church on Sundays. If I went, it was to Bible class and would flirt around with men at his church, in hopes one would run back and tell him; none did. Anthony has been kept away from me and out of my reach. None of his home boys would tell me anything and they wouldn't tote a message, just like the last time. I lost weight and didn't feel like living. I went on dates, but they weren't him. I hadn't had dick because my body only recognizes one dick. I've called and called throughout our separation and still no him. I was becoming frantic and not like me at all.

I found myself in a slump of depression and anxiety. Nothing mattered anymore and I didn't care. I couldn't care, although, I tried to go on but couldn't. I did not keep my boys much at all. When they are here, they stay a short while. They enjoyed Paisley's and I didn't mind. I can't get myself together with them here. I stooped low by calling as a telemarketer or a blocked number. That didn't work. I bought a prepaid phone and called sometimes and still no answer. I was at the end of ideas and wearing down. On this day, I tried calling

Anthony and it went to voicemail. A few hours later, I called him again and it went again to voicemail. A few more hours later I called, and he did not pick up. I kept blowing up his phone and texting him blank messages.

This time I left a message saying, "You may not answer my calls, but you will answer your front door."

In the middle of the night, my phone rang. I saw it was Anthony. My hands shook as I speedily answered the phone. He spoke, "What is it, Ley?"

"I don't get the words I miss you."

The line was quiet again as he asked, "What do you want?"

"Just to see how you are doing."

"I am doing ok. Have the boys made it back home?"

How he know they are not here? I thought. Instead, I stated, "They still at Paisley's."

"Tell them I will drop by and see them tomorrow."

"Tomorrow?"

"Yeah. Hadley has me tied up with functions after functions. She starts her new shift tomorrow and I can stop by then."

"I can't wait to see you."

"Yeah."

We hung up and my soul rejoiced. He is coming by to see us. I was happy again. I started picking out what to wear and playing in my mind how it all would go. He answered my call and for whatever reason I was glad. The sound of his voice brought back the happiness we once shared. I could only imagine what he has on and what he is doing. Verbally, I rejoiced. "Lord, thank you for letting us talk again." I made up my mind and went to sleep.

The next day I was surprised I went to sleep as I awoke early. He didn't say what time and if I know him, it'll be later. With all the excitement, I forgot the boys were at Paisley's. I could go and get them, but I am not. I must reel my man back in and the children would only take the spotlight off me getting him back. I fidget with calling him and asking the time, but it didn't matter. Whenever he arrives, he will only find me here, ready and easy.

Time was not going fast enough. The outfit I picked out was a short, flexible skirt with no panties of course, just in case he wants me like I crave him. I don't know how things are going between them. He hasn't said a word or kept in contact. However, I did tell him I wouldn't contact him, but I couldn't help it. I needed to hear from him, and I did. Sitting down in my living room was a huge job. I kept running to the sound of each car pulling in the complex. I was become a wreck waiting to happen.

After waiting all day and half the night, I had gotten tired and disappointed. I told Paisley to keep the boys till the weekend. She knew I needed time alone in handling this predicament. I didn't think he was going to show up, and then the knock came. My heart skipped some as I asked with anticipation, "Who is it?"

"Anthony."

I opened the door and his cologne hit me first. I moved out the way and he came in as I closed the door. I turned around, he grabbed and kissed me. I swear I fainted from his touch. My love said, "I've missed you."

"I missed you too."

He put his hands on my waist and felt my naked ass. He asked, "Are the boys still at Paisley's?"

"Yes, how did you know?"

"Shush and bend over. I haven't had this good pussy in a minute."

I didn't waste time. I leaned over the couch arm and put my face in the seat. I lifted my legs up. Anthony eased himself inside me and paused for a moment. I locked my legs behind his waist with a little room for moving. He kept standing there with his dick hung in me, not moving or speaking. I love how he does that. To me, he is taking it all in. He said, "I missed this pussy. Let me show you how much."

Anthony was going slow and deep. He was pushing all of him and me. I was crying and calling for him. My love was on his tiptoes and pressing me hard on the couch arm. He was punishing my pussy for being absent from him. My love was crushing me relentlessly into the couch. He kept saying, "Oooh. Shit now."

He was making love to me from the back and my pussy was happier than I was. The way he kept giving it to me made my body bounce hard. He was drawing back far and pushing it in me with each entry unfathomable. He was penetrating more than my vagina. He had touched my spirit, my brain. My Anthony was doing this like only he can. It didn't take long for him to go fast and hard in the pussy. Before he reached his peak, he stopped, and I didn't like that. I asked, "What's wrong?"

"I am not ready to nut, but damn, I can't keep this up."

"She needs you to fill her up."

He didn't say another word as he started back rocking and rubbing my face in the couch. He was out of control as he kept his hands all over my firm ass. He didn't want to stop, and I didn't want him to either. My own orgasm was silent as I buried my screams in the couch. I hadn't nut from the back in a long time and right now I loved the feel. As for my love, he said, "I see you leaking, but I can fix that."

Chapter 9

He swayed me like a mother rocking her child to sleep, as he rocked me from one side while holding one side little longer, making me feel how sturdy and complete he makes me. This man I love was extending my orgasms although it was long finished. My lover kept shaking me and thrilling me to death. He would speed up and slow down; speed up and slow down, by holding himself and not containing the good feeling. His nut was strange and funny. It didn't feel like his ordinary nut.

It was different and indescribable. It may be the way I was placed, and his nut has a better angle. Be that as it may, if I had a uterus, it would be preparing for a baby. Anthony kept standing behind me and my legs didn't fall. I wanted him in me if I could keep him there me. For some reason, it was important for his nut to linger and hang in there inside me. He patted my ass and I giggled. He said, "I have always loved the way your ass shook. But baby, you got to let me come up out this pussy."

"What if I don't want you to?"

"Then I will be forced to come back and get it again, and again, and again."

We laughed. I lifted my legs in the air with my head face down. He sat on the couch and asked, "What are you doing?"

I got up and straddled him. Not for sex but for comfort. I buried my head into his moist shirt and spoke, "I love you and I don't want to lose you again."

"I know you love me but you did tell me to try and work it out with Hadley."

"Then why are you here?"

"You have been on my damn mind. I can't stop thinking about you and your smile. The way you laugh and the boys; God, how I missed them" he spoke with sincerity.

"You miss me and can't stop thinking about me."

"I held out as long as I could that's why I ran here. I must see your beautiful face. If I had time, I would eat the pussy and carry your scent back with me."

"You don't know how good this feels to me. I thought you had left me alone completely."

"No. I can't ever do that. She thinks I am talking to another woman, and you are no longer a factor."

"I'm not?"

"No."

"Are you seeing anyone else? It's bad enough I share you with her. I don't need another woman trying to fuck this up."

"No. I am sold out for you."

"What does this mean? I mean can you come see me and spend time with me? If you can't, at least talk to me and let me know you still love me."

"I'll start sending messages through Paisley. I don't really trust my homeboys. They may try to fuck you and I'll fuck them up for that. Your great pussy ass is mine and I can't share you with another man."

"Why is that? I am sharing you."

"I was taken when you met me. I been hearing about you talking to men at church."

"All that is just talk. Keep me in your life and you won't have to share me."

"I will. I won't go this long without fucking you ever again, you hear me?"

"I hear you. Will I see you, since she's not focused on me, but on another imagination?" I spoke with laughter.

"I'll let Paisley know tomorrow" he said as he inhaled my skin to say, "You smell so sweet, Ley."

"I love the pet name you have given me. It sounds so right. Anthony, please stay the night with me. I want to hold you."

"Aren't you holding me now?"
Blushing like a schoolgirl in front of her crush, I said, "You know what I mean."

"I do," he spoke as he kissed my forehead.

Anthony left me that day. Just like he promised, he let Paisley know and she would let me know he was coming over. I became very happy. She would keep my boys when Anthony would come over so we could talk. Over half the time our encounters consisted of sexing like animals mating. I couldn't get enough of him. I would always make him do more than two nuts; therefore, if she wanted dick she would only get a sprinkle.

I was making it known he and his dick were all mine, even if he went home to her. In time, I would have the heart again. For now, I was content with what I was getting and what we had been doing. I let him take me any way he wanted and how ever long he wanted. His dick inside me made him crazy and unstoppable. I, on the other hand, loved it. He was taking time out for me and doing more things for me. Anthony started paying my small bills and buying me flowers and small gifts.

He would surprise me and not tell Paisley, claiming he wants to show up unannounced in case she was doing the same thing for me to another man. He knows he is the only one, but I let him think whatever because he goes away to another woman, every time he leaves me. Sometimes the crying would stop and for the most, it wouldn't. I could not lie. It does bother me knowing he is going home to his wife. Holding her and sexing her like he does me. Those ideas would rattle me because he loves to have his arms around me as we sleep. If he is this way with me, I know he is the same way with her.

Why can't she just leave again? The idea of running her off came to me as I slept one night. It was not the best idea, but I was happier while she was out the picture. This lady has no idea how much her husband means to me. He is three of the reasons why I live and the main reason, I can't let go of what we shared. Each time he and I are together, he tells me she has started back with the bullshit. This time it wasn't about me. He says, "She's fucked up and I'm beginning to hate ever being back with her."

I know he is coming because she doesn't satisfy him like I do. She doesn't know the man she married like I do. And yes, she doesn't take care of him like I can. He knows it and soon she will too, but she can't ever know I played a part. Then again, if she is on the bullshit like he says, she will do it herself. I have her blocked on social media; therefore, seeing my picture is impossible to her. On a few occasions, I would go on her job and ask about her. No one had an ill word to say about her.

From what I could tell, his wife was a model citizen. Her only problem was being there for everyone but her husband. She is dedicated to helping people and I saw that right away from the times I've observed her. The main reason, I am doing this is to find out why he can't leave her. Once a CNA said, "Dr. Vaughn is the only doctor who gives to charities and helps in the community and if a patient can't pay, she gets the hospital to do a write off."

I wanted to hear terrible things, but I didn't. If I wasn't in love with her husband, I would like her, but negative. I would rather love and fuck her husband than be anything to her. If it hadn't been for her husband, my children and I would be dead now. The man she married has given me purpose and reasons to tough it out. My thoughts asked me, *"How can you let go of a man who is your everything?"* my verbal reply was, "You can't and I won't."

My life has improved, and I'm not depressed anymore. Even my relationship with my twin was better. She told me she was in love with someone like Anthony, who is also married. I've never seen them together because I've been too busy being with Anthony as much as I could. On this day Paisley called me and asked, "You still want me to carry the baby for you?"

I hadn't forgotten, but with me not seeing my love, I didn't think it would still be possible. Being overjoyed, I exclaimed, "Yes. It would mean so much for me if you do."

"Well, I ovulate tomorrow. You have to get his nut in a condom and give it to me."

"You know sperm dies fast. How can you get it real fast?"

"I will be in the boy's room. You get the condom and bring it to me. Can you do it?"

"I will try. He will know something is up

because he never fucks me with a condom."

"Y'all fuck raw?" she asked, surprised.

"All the time and if you had the dick, you would want it raw too," I added.

"Anyway, I will come over before he gets there and hide."

"Thank you so much for doing this for me. I believe this will bring him and I back as a family."

"I hope so, twin, you deserve it."

"Who got the boys?"

"I will let a friend I trust watch them. I will say I need to run over to your house for a few to pick up the boys some clothes or something. He will buy it."

"Okay. See you tomorrow night."

"Okay. Bye, Ainsley."

We got off the phone and my mind went haywire. I was ecstatic about her carrying the baby. I'm going to be a mom again, but this time to a real man who loves me. A little while later, Anthony called me. I told him I want to use a condom and he asked why. I told him I have a bladder infection. He bought it. I lay in bed and laughed with my thoughts, this man has been there for me and yet he is so easy. He takes me over his wife, and he believes what I tell him. I make good ass love to him, and he keeps coming back. I'm not trying to break up his home, but the foundation is already cracked and falling to the ground. Why not be there to pick him up when he needs someone? A bladder infection? I laughed again.

I slept like a baby that night. All day, I was over excited and anxious. I got up and took a bath. I made sure my body oil was shiny and smelling. He loves the way I smell, and I love him smelling me. I put on a robe and Paisley came over she said, "Don't be too long or loud. I don't want to hear you fucking in there. Make him nut quick. Ok?"

"Okay."

At that moment, I saw his car pull up. She hid in the boy's bathroom as I opened the door. He handed me flowers and a present. I closed the door. The first question he asked was, "I saw Paisley's car. Is she here?"

"No. She got a friend to pick her up."

"Oh. It better not be a friend for you."

"It's not," I spoke with a warm smile.

Anthony handed me the present and said, "Open it."

I opened it and saw a ring. I looked at him and asked, "What is this?"

"It's a promise ring."

I took it out the box and asked with a surprise, "What are you promising?"

"I am promising to be only yours and keep you in my heart."

"Are you for real?" I was shocked.

"I am. I told you to give me some time,"

"What brought this on?"

"We know each other for well over a year and no one has come close to you."

Those words did not reach my ears fast enough until I heard something bump. I knew it was Paisley. He stopped and asked, "What was that?"

"Let me go look."

I went in the boy's room, and she gave me the hurry it up sign. I came out and spoke, "I didn't see anything." He sat on the couch, and I asked, "Do you have time for a quickie?"

"You know we fuck, it's never really a quickie."

"Well, I have a bladder infection. I don't want you to get it," I responded, knowing he can't get it like that. I hope he buys it.

Anthony stared at me and spoke. "Yeah, I can do that. There's a first time for everything."
I handed him the extra-large Magnum rubber. He was already hard as he slid it on. He said, "I'm hitting it doggie style."

I didn't want Paisley to see just how hung Anthony is, because I know she's peeping. Putting myself in another position, he asked, "Why you get right there?"

"I don't know."

"Get right here."

He picked a place where she could see how long his strokes could be. I didn't like that, but I need him to nut quick. Not debating any longer, I got in the position he wanted and lifted my robe while getting on all four limbs. I parted my legs and lifted my ass to greet Mr. Good Dick. Anthony slid into me with ease. His stride was different. He was acting like he was in a porn movie. I know he can't see Paisley peeping, but I could.

To act out, I hollered like they do in such flicks. I even kept looking back at him to see his face. Anthony was getting into it and making my ass giggle. He held onto my hips and kept hitting me like it was the best piece of pussy ever and I loved it. My Anthony was rolling and hitting me so hard, my arms kept buckling. That did not stop him. He went closer to the floor with me. After a few more minutes of grinding and rocking me side to side, he exploded with the loudest sound ever. He held onto the condom and eased out of me. I got up as he stayed on all his knees. Sweat was racing down his chest as he said, "Here, get rid of it."

I got the condom. He got up and fixed his pants. I handed the condom to her. I got him a towel and closed the door. When I came back, he was sleep. Thirty minutes later, Paisley eased the door open and came out. She gave me the thumbs up. I closed the front door and sat there. Soon as he woke up, we talked like old times before all the sex. I really enjoyed it. In all honesty, I enjoy this more than all things else.

To some degree, an odd sensation overcame me. He went to the bathroom. I got his phone and saw quite a few texts from some other woman. I know he's not cheating on me! The unread text read: bring the good dick to me when you finish playing with her. I text back: you sure you want this dick she replied: Shit yeah!

I erased the texts and sat back motionless. He came out the bathroom. He saw me and asked, "You okay?"

"I'm good."

"You don't act like it."

"Got a lot on my mind."

Anthony really didn't buy what I said. He glared at me and took what I said at face value. Not paying any attention to my body language, he said oddly, "Well, I have to be going. I have another stop to make."

"Where's that?"

"I told Hadley I was going to bring her some strawberries."

Somehow that statement bothered me, and he knew it. My love spoke, "Not like that. She wanted some and I told her I would run out and get them. I didn't say I was running by here to get some good pussy from you."

He gave me a heartfelt hug and I felt safe. I didn't want to let him go and he held on to me. He left quickly after our embrace. I took a wash off and went to bed. I could not sleep. I kept thinking how I needed to get my life together and change. So far, all I been doing is fucking Anthony and panting behind him like a puppy. My life seems to be a revolving door with nothing going well. Sure, I have the man I love, but he can't offer me his last name or his total honesty.

I feel as if I am settling, complacent and not really satisfied. If I could leave him alone I would. I have tried and it did not work. This man has me under water and I can't swim. It makes no sense how hooked he has me. The song, "I Just Can't Stay Away From You" by En Vogue is so true in my life. There is something about him that keeps me coming back.

I know it is not right to love him as I do, but I can't help it. I wouldn't want my husband to be friends with a woman like me, but I expect her to like it. I am sneaky, conniving, cunning and everything else, but I have a good heart. I don't try to use my beauty, but for a long time it was all I had. Now I use it at will because I don't want my true, low and degrading self-esteem showing. I took a sigh and continued to stare at the ceiling. The only thing on my mind is doing right, but how? I see now there must be another woman and my heart broke. I cried relentlessly at the thought of him with some else. I have given him my all and each time I tried letting him go, I couldn't.

The tears kept falling nonstop. This hurt worse than him leaving me alone the first time. I can't allow this pain in my chest to continue grabbing my eyes. My conscience questioned me and dealt with me, sternly chastising me. "You really can't find love in another woman's husband. He could treat you like gold and show you off as a trophy, but marrying you is out the question. Things always start off as friendly, but he told you how the line was crossed before the first time you gave it to him. He told you he can't offer you any more than what you have and yet; you allowed him to lead you by the nose.

On many occasions, he kept stating he won't leave his wife and you made a conscientious decision on staying around. Before your feelings got in the way you had running time. Presently, your heart is missing, and you lost. Sin makes itself look and feel so good. If it were bad looking or feeling, no one would choose it. Anthony is sin to you, so ask yourself how can he be faithful to you, and he's married? What makes you think you were the only one? You were about to kill yourself before you met him; consequently, he sees you as a piece of ass he gets. He didn't tell you to fall for him; you did that on your own.

You weren't satisfied until you tricked him into wanting you. You could have turned down any advance he made, but you didn't. You were happy his wife left for a moment, and you took him right in. You took in almost everything she had been dealing with and you didn't heed her warning. Nevertheless, another woman is taking your place because you tried taking the wife's place. However, the wife is not included because she is legally his, while you all want to be his. You don't think his wife was hurt by you being dishonest in your motives with her husband? Hadley didn't know what she was talking about by calling you out on your crap, nor did she?

He didn't believe her because he wanted to fuck you and stop other men from wanting you. This man you love is your perfect imperfection. He is everything you want but nothing you need. He is just as guilty as you are and for that, the price becomes high. If you were tuned in to God, you would have seen how she was helping you. You got mad and denied her truths. Sure, you have a heart, but what about her heart when it came to you and her husband? His loyal wife may not be there for him like you think because you listens or understands him, but the truth is she is his wife. He married her for a reason and there's a reason Jesus has them still together.

You stated how you've lost all respect for her. The truth is, you never had it or wanted it. You believe your own lies and that makes you very dangerous, and in serious trouble. Even the man in the park all those months ago told you about yourself; again, you did not receive warning. No one wants awful things happening in their life, but what do you think is to happen for the wrongdoing you did in that marriage? Don't say you didn't do anything. You did. You called his house, cell phone and sent numerous messages through various people. You also told lies in making conversations with him. You had him ignoring his wife for you and you talked to his wife as if she was his girlfriend.

Ainsley, you added your children because you knew he has a soft spot for the boys. You cried fake tears about made-up situations you were experiencing and all for what? My dear you pulled every trick known to man. You didn't care about any one feeling but yours. You couldn't care less who it hurt or angered. You only cared about this man in your life. The worst thing you did was lie on Jesus. You stated you believe Jesus brought you in their marriage to bring them together. That is far from the truth, and you know it.

It matters not if he came after you, you should have let him be, but you didn't. Being his friend will cost you more than you are willing to lose if you don't do your part and end it. That wife of his more likely has a lot of tears, time and prayers invested in her marriage. That is why she is still a major player in the game. She is not going to just let you, or any other woman, come in and take what she has built. It is time consuming once you've been with someone, to give them your all, just for them to hurt you.

You are crying real tears now and those could have been spared if you had listened. You have discovered another woman has been added to this mess and what can you do about it? He already cheating and he isn't yours. Ask yourself, was falling for another woman's husband worth the pain you are feeling right now? You are confusion and most definitely will pay. Making up my mind for good, I said to God, "Lord, meeting Anthony was for a reason. He showed me what I need, and I hate he is married, but I love him. Lord, I love him and because of that, please give me your strength to leave the man I love, because I can't do it in my own strength."

Chapter 10

A little over two weeks passed and still no word from Paisley. She has not talk to me since I picked up the boys. Anthony hasn't contacted me, and I am undecided if I want him. Lately at night, I hadn't been able to sleep. But tonight, I fell asleep and didn't know it. I awoke with a missed call from Anthony. I didn't call him back, right away. For a minute now, my conscience has placed a lot on me. I got up, took the boys back to Paisley and I laid back down. She acted strange as I drop the boys off. I assumed it's because of her friend.

My thoughts were cluttering my head and I could not get out of bed. Then my flesh got the best of me. I called Anthony back. He answered, "Hello."

"I had a missed call from you."

"I must have pocket dialed you."

"Pocket dialed?"

"Yeah, I am at Paisley's with my home boy. I have your boys outside while they finish up from being busy inside. You want to come over? I can fry some fish and fries. It would be fun."

My first thought was, *when he started going out with a homeboy? Better yet... why is he at my sister's house with his homeboy?* I didn't ask any questions, I just stated, "No. I want to be alone."

"Whoa. You okay?"

He knows something is up. I have never missed an opportunity to be with him, ever since we have known each other; friendly and sexually. I tried hiding my feelings by saying, "I am. I just think we don't need to see each other anymore."

"What?"

"I don't think," was all I said because the phone lost service. I didn't call him back. I got up and took a shower. I came out my bathroom. Anthony was there. He scared me, and I hollered. He sounded angry as he yelled, "What the hell you mean; you think we shouldn't see each other anymore?"

"I just don't think we should. You are married and probably have other women. I don't need that or this, in my life anymore. In fact, this has gone on

206

over two years too long. I've lost my heart and soul to another woman's husband, and I shouldn't. I need my own man, but I can't have him if I am hung up over you."

He came towards me and said, "The message you saw was not for me. My homeboy had used my phone to text his ole girl. I only have you and Hadley. Right now, I have you."

The love in my eyes must have showed dim. Anthony walked a little closer and said with love in his mouth, "Don't do this to me, Ley. I love you. I can't take it if you leave me alone. Don't keep you from me."

I didn't want to hear it. I walked away as he snatched me around. My robe came down. A few seconds passed and neither of us reacted. He glared at my skin before kissing me. I tried fighting him, but I couldn't. He was stronger and more determined. Once he had me in his grip, all the blood in my heart made me more aggressive. I resisted him as covered me with rough, yet soft kisses. His solid arms held me in his clutches as his mouth found my breasts in the middle of the resisting. However, I still fought him, but his mouth snatched my nipple and melted me in his arms.

The disagreement was over, and he was winning. I could no longer hold him off from what I really wanted him to have. My mind screamed no, but my body was hollering, yes oh yes. This man is crack, and I am a highly addicted drug addict. It seems true, the longer I stay away from him the more I had to have him. There is no antidote in sight and no cure for me. On my end, everything was happening so fast. We didn't make it to the bed. We didn't get on the floor. He had me against the wall with one leg on his shoulder and the other one around his waist.

He was grunting and acting like this was the last time he would get it; hence, he was not holding back the loving. This man is recalling why we have chemistry Other than the communication, our sex is always phenomenal. Any position he places me in, is surely mind-blowing and extraordinary good. This thing under my nose let out a sexual panting in his ear, while I heard his deep husky breath in mine.

His manner by itself created an erotic tension like stepping on gum and pulling your feet from it. Unquestionably this day, I'm saturated and sticking to him. Nothing relates to the rough housing he is giving me. My body doesn't care how sore it will be after this because he was making up for it. The animal who takes me is going subterranean inside me with his man probe. I almost wish I had my legs around him to lock him.

Anthony had his eyes closed as he kept running me into the wall. I know this is wrong, but wrong feels so right. He feels so good and he gives me a feeling like no other. My man used one last stance and smashed his hardened body into me. His orgasm was long as he bit down on my ear and sucked on it. He has never done that before, I thought as I closed my eyes. I didn't want him to see I was watching him and thinking the entire time. He moved some and I let my leg down. He eased me back on my feet and said, "You can't stop me from loving you or being here for you and the boys."

My lover pulled me close to him and held me for about five minutes. He is acting differently, I thought as I waited for him to move. Once he did, he pulled up his pants and said, "Each time we make love, I don't want to come out of you. Ainsley, you have me hooked and I know you know you do."

"If I had you hooked, you would be with me and I would be your wife."

Anthony kissed me and said, "Who says you aren't going to be my wife soon? You do wear my promise ring."

I lowered my head because he was truthful. I still wear his ring. I asked, "Well, time waits for no one, and I am getting older. A promise ring is just a promise ring, and not a wedding band."

"You been waiting this long, what's a little while longer?"

He was right again. I said, "Why you come over here for anyway?"

"You were talking about leaving me alone

and I couldn't have that. You are the only woman in my life next to Hadley. But with you, I have a real relationship. I have a real marriage with you."

"You told me she thinks there is some other woman."

"She does think that."

"I would think the same way. Well, what was I to think when I saw that text?"

"Shit. I have a wife and she bugs the fuck out of me. Don't you start on shit that doesn't concern me or you?"

He had an attitude. I got one too. "I don't want to be looking like a fool either. It's bad enough I'm madly in love with a married man. I don't need a married Casanova, Don Juan, Romeo or whatever fits. If I can't be the main woman, I should be the only woman."

With a snug tone, he stated flatly and truthfully, "You right. I want my own son and you can't have kids. Ain't a damn baby coming out of you, but shit."

Those true words burned and stung. He saw

the water in my eyes. He knows my reasons, and now my reasons are his reasons for not being with me. I asked with a funky attitude, "So all I have become to you is a good fuck?"

"No. You are more than that, but sometimes the fuck's not as good as the head."

I felt like shit. If he was making this hard for me, it worked. "You just threw up in my face about children and how my head game is sometimes better than my pussy."

"Did I lie?"

"I don't know if you did or not."

"Then why you mad?"

"Because if I could carry your baby, I would, besides I am already on it."

"On what?"

I felt as if I shouldn't say a word, but the door is open, and he might as well know. The joy I was expressing overlapped to him by saying, "I've asked Paisley to carry your baby for me."

"What?"

"Paisley has agreed to carry your baby for

me."

"How is that?"

"I had your nut put in a condom and she artificially inseminated herself with your nut."

He was quiet as he said, "You did that, the night you claimed there was a bladder infection, didn't you?"

"Yes."

"Paisley watched me fuck you, didn't she?" he asked in a strange way.

"Yes. Are you mad?"

Anthony was beyond mad.

"Let me see. Instead of you letting me put the nut in you, you put my nut in your sister."

"Yes."

"BITCH! I am still married. So, what do you suggest I tell my wife about your sister having my baby, if she conceives?"

Damn, I didn't think about that. I assumed he and I would be together, but we aren't. I spoke the truth. "I really thought we would be together and how Hadley feels would not be our concern. Since

Paisley and I are twins, and share the same DNA, the baby would have a lot of me in it as well. I did it out of love, or so I thought."

"Love? You did what out of love?"

The way he said it sounded like hate with passion. I tried explaining with words, "I wanted a part of you, and having any part of you drove me to do this. I would have done it, but as you pointed out to my face, I can't have kids. I know you would be a great dad. I see how you are to the boys."

"But I am still married! Have you forgotten that part?" he screamed.

I have never seen him so angry in my life. He acted dizzy as he looked around to have a seat. He didn't sit down. He stormed out my bedroom. I went behind him. He made it to the living room, and I rushed to the front door. I blocked it. He said, "Get out of my way. I have to get out of here."

"Anthony, I love you. Baby, I love you. I did this for us."

The love of my life didn't hear my love for him. His next words stung. "You better hope it didn't work."

He yanked me out the way and I fell on the couch. He flung the door open and stormed out as the door slammed behind him. I got up and closed it while crying. The tears would not stop. I really thought he would be happy, but he wasn't. I don't know what to. But I did use my phone and call Paisley. She answered the phone and I told her about Anthony. She didn't really say much. However, she did say it would be a few more days, if not a week before she goes for the day twenty-one test; then again, she might wait until she missed a period.

Today was the first time in a very long time; I felt a fate worse than dying. The look in his eyes spoke of hate and hatred. I don't know if that is possible, but that's what was in the glare he gave me. I pondered deeply into my life. He will have that part of me, no matter what we go through. I got back in the shower and just stood there and thought, in the book of Ezekiel chapter thirty- six and verse twenty- five says, "Then I will sprinkle clean water on you." I was trying to let the water wash me clean and right again, before all the evil, vindictive, cruel and undermined things I'd started doing to Hadley's marriage through her husband.

If I could change it, I would have just stayed his friend and not gotten involved in his marriage. In part, I know how his wife felt when she found out about me falling in love with him. I did blame her, but I did have a part; a small part is still a part. I could not help it. He found me and I was desperate. In a way, if I never started flirting with danger, I wouldn't be in this trouble now, but I can't change what has happened. I don't think I would want to change because Anthony has been a huge part of my life.

You can't tear off a chunk of you and not notice it. That is how he is to me. My imperfect philosophy was altered by the man I called my best friend and for the longest time, he was my only friend. I saw I could use my ability of persuasion on him, which made me think he and I could really have a future. He was unhappy with his life and wife. I was beyond disbelief in mine. This man I fell for changed all the negative things about me into positive. This man in my life has stabilized all my unbalanced situations, from the lack of love to the incest. He knows all things about me, and I played my pain on his emotions.

I just used it the wrong way. Now I think I have lost him because of my trickery. I really didn't mean any harm. Now I am wondering could I feel the same way if I was the wife and Hadley was the outside woman who wanted to take my place. I physically shook my head no. I would be angrier than she is. I would kill me and cut me to sunder for being involved with my husband. I would not be as kind as she has been to me. I would find her and beat the shit out of her, but Hadley hadn't done that to me. She has been quiet; too quiet, not making any noise about me and her husband. She has been the opposite and that's a warning sign.

I sighed because the Word says, 'Destruction cometh.' I could not remember the rest, so I found it in Ezekiel chapter seven verse twenty-five.

'Destruction cometh; and they shall seek peace, and there shall be none.' I have no idea what that meant. But I knew it meant I must attend church. You can say I had quit going because church people were the same everywhere.

Getting in the shower, I became aware how I thought my Anthony was different, yet he was almost the same. I remembered my life choices, like how I used to attend this church. All the men kept up appearances while having every kind of imaginable sex with me, while their wives were out of town or too busy for their husband. Some of the deacon's tag teamed me, and I didn't care.

Every time I get two at one time, it's usually all-night. Those church men act like they don't know how to quit reaching orgasms. They would get a nut each with me sucking on the other one. These men were real freaks and sneakier than anyone. For the most, their wives were uptight, snobby bitches who looked down on women like me. The truth is, its women like me that keep their men pleased so they can stay married longer.

These men know I am clean, and I don't run my mouth. They always gave me whatever I needed. Half the time, my regulars would only play in my pussy and suck on my nice breasts. Many would admire me and tell me how elegant and put together I am. They flattered me and tried all kinds of things with me, then would go home and do it. I didn't make them feel ashamed of what they were trying to do. I allowed these men to explore their hidden dreams of what real sex with a woman they love should be like.

I've had threesomes with a deacon and his wife. I've had foursomes with two deacons and their wives. I was showing them how to sexually please their husbands. I must admit, sometimes it was uncomfortable letting them see me suck their husband's dicks, but I assured them, this was just an act, and I didn't want their men. They went along with it.

Sometimes their husbands would meet me at a hotel, and we would have sex for hours, or until he couldn't take it anymore. My body had gotten me and out a lot of things and it still could. The new me I wants to stop. Unfortunately, my family found out about my lifestyle and banned me.

They didn't show me what I needed, and I was getting loved and attention from everyone but them. I was out there and being well taken care of, despite my diabetes and low self-esteem. On many occasions, I would be the stripper at a bachelor party and end up fucking the groom or making him nut all over my perky breasts. I've had one groom, who only wanted anal sex because he really liked men. I didn't ask why he was getting married, because I knew the marriage was for show.

One night a man on his honeymoon and we met me at the bar. His wife had sea sickness and we hit it off. He told me he was an evangelist, and he had a Word from the Lord. Well, that Word ended him up in my room and riding him like a cowgirl. He kept his wedding ring on, and I don't know why. Throughout the entire trip, he would sneak off and sex me like I was his wife. His loving was so good and so wonderful. I would get mad whenever he went back to his room. This man was wild in the bedroom and he made me feel special. He made me feel loved and for the last duration of the trip, he had quit fucking me. He started making love to me. He told me, I needed to feel what making love felt like.

He did that. He made love to me for four nights in a row, all night long. He has stayed the night on our final nights. I would wake up and suck him for breakfast. During the day, he would eat me for lunch. He was unique. He spoiled me before screwing me. He bought flowers, candy and wine. I had asked what his wife thought about him being gone during these two weeks, while she laid up sick. He had said he told her he would be in the chapel praying and sometimes he fell asleep on his knees.

It amazed me how gullible most church women are about their churchgoing husbands. When we left the ship, I was very sad. My time with him showed me if a man is married and he falls for a woman like me, there is no honesty in the marriage or upcoming marriage. Personally, married men and church men was all that attracted me. I don't know why, but if he wasn't married or went to church, I didn't want him. I assumed it's because I was in the church all the time and if he has God in him, then how could it be wrong?

In one church, I was going with the preacher, and he ended up leaving his family. But when he left them, he soon left me by cheating on me with another woman of another church. These two men in the church, they ruined the idea of faithful men of God. But Anthony changed it. He didn't see me as a trophy. He didn't see me as a pussy or head game. He saw me as a woman with a past. No man has ever just seen me as a human being. He never came at me. He was just a friend, but I had to see if he was like all the men I had in my past.

It took a while. Some part of me believes if his wife wasn't on him about me, he would never look at me as a woman. He kept our conversations light; although, I kept throwing sexual hints out at him. Once he started flirting back and lying just to come see me; I knew I had him. He was the only man I had intentionally gone after in hopes to have a future. Soon as things started getting serious, I welcomed it. I was not disappointed because I had fallen in love with him.

He was different from all the other men. He didn't go to church a whole lot, but says his wife has more faith than him. For him to be there for me whenever, gave me weight. I knew then, I would not stop fucking him. If he left me alone, I would go after him. He is just as much my love as he is hers. The difference is he completes me with the bond we have.

Chapter 11

Thinking no more, I got out the shower after trying to wash away my sins. I dried off and went to bed. I didn't want to think of anything anymore. I have done too much of that. Tomorrow, I will go to a church and hear what God says. I am restless of the way things have gone. Nothing I have done has worked. I am tired of the life I am living and wish for something diverse. My boys need a father and I need a husband. I see I can't get that in Anthony; I see that now. He already belongs to Hadley; I was just borrowing him and understanding now I need my own.

The next day I awoke, with a smile. I opened the newspaper to the list of churches. I closed my eyes and counted to twenty. The minute I opened my eyes, my finger pointed on an old fashion tent revival in another part of town with the last night being tonight. How perfect is that? I thought. I asked Paisley if she wanted to attend. She told me no, but she'd keep the boys while I used her car. I got off the phone with her and got sick. *This is the devil trying to get me out of not going,* I thought.

I took my diabetic medicine, had some crackers and a Sprite. I felt a lot better. My sister got her friend to drop her car off for me and I started on my way. As the trip began, I watched the scenery change. Things in this area seemed happier and homely. It's funny how I grew up in this county and now visiting a part of town I never knew existed. The houses screamed love and the people's attitude were upbeat. I could move here and get away from Hadley and Anthony, I thought as I found the small tent revival.

Parking was free and the place was half-full. I got out and sat in the middle of older women. The energy was high in this place. The music was alive in me. I found myself clapping and feeling free. My feelings no longer existed. That affair with Anthony became second place. I did not have a care in the world. I never felt so relieved in all my days. Soon as we all settled, the woman came forth. She was tanned in color, and short in stature but her voice carried a lot of weight as she yelled, "God is not finished with you! Get up and praise him now!"

All around me people were jumping and clapping people. Many of the women were waving their hands and agreeing. The small children were in on the joyful mood. The ushers gathered the children and sat them down. The older women all became solemn. I sat with them and listened, "Let us pray. God the Father, we know you sent Jesus the son to die for us. He came out from you to be seen of man just for man to be redeemed. We ask you to heal the land and send down your holy Word. Lamb of God, I ask for wisdom. I ask you to guide my mouth when it comes to speaking to your people. Thank you, Lord, for letting it be done, in the mighty most precious name of Jesus Christ, Amen."

We all agreed with the Word, "Amen." The lady spoke with authority, "I am going to bring forth the Word of God about God, Amen."

Some agreed while others nodded. I sort of let my eyes linger low. I didn't want her to call me out because I know if God tells a real woman or man of God something, they must tell you. I figure, if she doesn't see me, she can't tell me anything about my sin. It would be embarrassing if that happens. I know I am a sinner who has fallen far from glory. I don't need anyone telling me what I am doing is wrong. I asked for a fan to hide behind. The lady gave me one and I fanned, slowly.

No one was talking. She had all the attention. The speaker said, "How can you describe an everlasting God to temporal people? Their minds won't grasp the magnitude of how forever God is. To defend God, you must first know who is God. HE must be everything to you; your sole existence and then some, Amen."

"Amen," I heard some say.

The woman stated, "Hebrews chapter seven verse two through three, states, 'To whom also Abraham gave a tenth part of all; first being by interpretation King of righteousness, and after that also King of Salem, which is, King of peace. Without father, without mother, without descent, having neither beginning of days nor end of life but made like unto the son of God; abideth a priest continually.' For Abraham to pay tithes, this man must be a great man. How could Abraham, a man of God pay tithes to a man who has neither beginning nor end? This Word tells you Melchisedec lived and never died. Just like God. He lives and never dies; however, the fleshly earthly part of God went to the grave in the name of Jesus and arose in three days. In the King James Version Bible, Mark chapter eight verse twenty-seven states, 'And Jesus went out, and his disciples, into the towns of Caesarea Philippi: and by the way he asked his disciples, saying unto them, Whom do men say that I am?' Stop right there. The Lord of Lords asked his circle who they think he is?' Sometimes you can be hanging around someone and not know who they are to you. You can have an idea, or maybe you don't know who it is you hanging around. It can go either way. Plenty of times we are just guessing and not knowing. People have their own definition of who God is. Verse twenty-eight says, 'And they answered, John the Baptist; but some say, Elias; and others, One of the prophets.' Stop right there. Unless HE becomes your personal Savior, you will go by what your grandmother says, what your mother says, or what people say. At this point, it's hearsay. You still don't know who God is. You can't expect get to know someone if you never talk or spend time with them. There must be some type of communicational, relationship going on to be with someone. If you don't talk to Christ, how can you expect to be involved with him? You are what's called a foreign bride, wanting rights to a man who's not yours. You must make the Lord yours for you are already HIS. Come unto the Lord for he desires a communion with you and be better to you than you are to yourself. Verse twenty-nine says, 'And he saith unto them, But whom say ye that I am? And Peter answereth and saith unto him, Thou art the Christ.' For Peter to say Thou art the Christ, he must have a personal relationship with him, and communication for him to know who God is to him. Many of us don't have a clue who God is nevertheless who Jesus really is. Who is God to you? Who is he in your life? Obtain the knowledge that God is light, and light in the scientific term means an electromagnetic radiation within a certain portion of the electromagnetic spectrum. God can be everywhere and with you all at once. You can't get rid of a God you can't naturally see; for light is said to be a natural agent that stimulates sight and makes things visible. You can't get rid of a God you physically can't touch. I mean you can't touch God himself, but you can touch the things created by God. God is energy and in physics, energy is property that must be transferred to an object for the object to perform work on, or to heat the object which can be converted in form, but not created or destroyed. God is water and water is a colorless, transparent, odorless, liquid that forms the seas, lakes, rivers, and rain and is the basis of the fluids of living organisms. Water also is called the universal solvent because it dissolves more substances than any other liquid. Understand, God is not man. HE can do anything and everything but fail; however, here are four things God can't do. One, HE can't stop existing because HE is eternal and has always existed before the beginning of time. Two, God can't be second. HIS Word says, 'Thy shalt have no other gods before me.' God does not want to come behind your job, your hobby, your family or your money. Three, God can't lie because lying brings forth sin and sin brings forth death. Number four, God can't sin because HE is a holy and just God. I am going to deal with sin for a moment. When you think about sin, you don't think of the unimportant things. Your mind gets focused on the massive things like, killing, stealing, lying, adultery, lusting, covering up for those in wrongdoings and fornicating, just to name a few. What about trickery? What about purposely being underhanded to someone who is an unwilling participate in your game? What about deceitful? Sure, Jacob, name means trickery, was deceitful towards his father about being Esau for the blessings of God. That which Jacob did was God ordained. But the stuff people do these days is not of God because they intentionally become dishonest, intentionally lie and betray people who mean them no harm. In this day and time, people have twisted God ordained to their way. They feel what they are doing as far as, creeping being involved in a marriage; they think they have done no wrong. A marriage is still a marriage; loveless or not. These interfering people believe their own lies by thinking, the man and wife are not living together, or they were already having problems. Anything great or small can be a factor in any relationship but if you are devious, wicked or anything other than honest in your intentions, you sin. That woman or man can offer you the moon, but if you know you don't need to be on the moon, you better not take it. The enemy will send you that special someone you been waiting on, just to get you in a mess, if not dead in your mess."

She looked like she was looking at me as she said through my spirit, "This is the last warning."

I could have melted through the ground and went to Hell right then and there. I felt those words when she said them. The breath left my lungs. My heart's thumping in my ear while my blood felt like it oozed out my body with each heartbeat. This preacher lady has spoken to my soul. Her tone was strong as it delivered those words. She could have been talking to someone behind me but if she was, I took it for me. Somehow, I zoned out and heard her say, "Over in Romans chapter six verse twenty-three it says, 'The wages of sin is death but the gift of God is eternal life through Jesus Christ our Lord.' The Word says in, Ezekiel chapter eighteen and verse twenty, 'The soul that sinneth shall die.' In James chapter one and verse fifteen, the Word says, 'Then when lust hath conceive, it brings forth sin and sin when it is finished, bring forth death.' According to the King James Version Dictionary, sin is a voluntary departure of moral agent from a known rule of rectitude or duty prescribed by God, any voluntary transgression of the divine law. People if you haven't learned, learn today. Nothing good ever comes after sin. Sin can cause you your life, and in some instances, the lives of those you love. One thing about sin is it doesn't stay where it started; it grows. Sin is nothing to play with, but some believe they can beat Satan at sin. Some think if I get out in time or my sin isn't like that. Wrong. All sin is like that. You may not have intentions, but sin doesn't stay as an intention. It can't be sin if it does. Sin lives in your flesh and in your flesh, is what you 'feel' is right. If you in a mess with sin, get out and get out fast. No sense of holding onto people who help keeps you out of a place with God. This maybe a tent revival, but this place is open for those who want to accept Jesus as their personal Savior. You don't have to be ashamed. HE loves you in your present state and will bless your spirit for your future state. HIS Word says, 'Come ye, all that labor and are heavy laden, and I will give you rest.' The Lord wants you to come to him so he may take away your burdens."

I did not get up at first. I waited for many people to make their way up front. I eased out the tent and sat in the car. My hands trembled with much fear. My thoughts were getting away with me and out of control. I could not gather my senses for the world. Having a broken spirit and a contrite heart, I cried. I am guilty of doing just what she said. I was verbally apologizing to God for my wrongdoings. Not using my better judgment, I called Anthony. He asked, "What's wrong with you?"

"I must confess," I spoke with tears and regret.

He was quiet as I said, "I used persuasion to have you with me. I mean I knew you would be there for me whenever I called. I knew you would choose listening to me over your wife, because all I had to do was be sad or need you. It never failed. You became my only support system and you showed me the love I had longed for. It was natural for me to want you and to need you in my life. I didn't mean to. I was selfish and wanting you to need me and not your wife, and you did. You were more of my husband than hers; you just wouldn't leave her for me."

"Whoa, settle down. Ley, pump your brakes."

"I must be honest. I have to be honest and confess my faults," I cried, tears and sadness punctuated my words.

"Listen, you can't make me do what I don't want to do. I don't care how good you use your words or how things went. If I didn't want to be there for you, I wouldn't. If I didn't want you, I wouldn't be with you."

"But you were married, and you thought I had hurt her, when I didn't."

"And I am still married. I don't want you and her fighting for nothing. Dry your eyes. There is no reason to cry."

"Should I call her and apologize for my involvement in your marriage? I want to do right," I asked sincerely.

"Hell no! Don't call my wife telling her shit about me and you. You don't apologize for shit. You hear me?"

"But Anthony—"

"Don't 'but Anthony' me!"

"She must forgive me for my part in your marriage and I have to ask for forgiveness."

"You didn't have any part about my marriage falling apart. It is all her fault for not being there when I needed her. Her fault for leaving me alone and leaving me. Just leave it alone. I got this."

"What if she tries to hurt me and my boys?"

"She won't do that. She too worried about her mother right now. And I am worried about you, and why you want to suddenly apologize for shit that has nothing to do with you. All this shit been brewing for years, long before you came along. So how the hell you gone temp me to do what the hell I want to do?"

Emotionally reiterating the reason why I called, I explained, "I believe I should talk to her. I must ask her to forgive me, and then ask God for forgiveness. The Bible says to ask forgiveness from the one you hurt, then go back to God and ask forgiveness from him. You told me that before."

"Didn't I tell yo ass, you don't have to say shit to her? I already told you that. Why you keep bringing up the same bullshit up? Hell, she's not with me. Do you not want to be with me during my time of need?"

"I don't want anything else, but to be with you. I just know I was a part of the confusion and damage to your marriage, intentionally or not. I should let her know I am very sorry."

He was scary quiet before saying, "I tell you what. Since you fucking act like you can't understand what I'm saying, listen. If you call her, I'm getting that ass and nobody gonna keep me off you. Is that clear?"

This time my line was quiet. I closed my

eyes and sighed. I don't know what else to tell him. I am distraught and have learned better. I know I have really and truly had evil intentions in his marriage. Ever since that lady spoke, 'That is the last warning" doing right has been the only thing on my mind. He played his part and I played mine. The difference is I was led by the flesh in my doings. This sinful flesh has caused me to have a wickedness manifested that I wanted to change but is still there.

Yes, I am guilty of making men leave their girlfriends, but not wives. My part in past marriages was affairs and going on about my business. But with this married man, I love him. I heard him ask me again, "Did you hear me?" I didn't answer and he knew I heard him, but he asked, "Where you at anyway?"

"I'm still at the tent revival. Where are you at?"

"I just arrived at your sister's."

"What you doing there?"

"I plan on getting the boys and meeting you at your house."

"Well, how you not know where I was?"

"You know I know your whereabouts," he said as to see if I would be honest with him.

"I don't know what you know," I stated softly.

"You know I am the only man who can hold

you just right."

"That I do know."

"Well. Get off this phone and drive careful."

I hung up and drove to my house quickly. Why is he picking up my boys for me? Why am I falling back with him, when I just heard the Word? What is he doing at my sister's? When has he started going over there and not to mention, he never said anything about his homeboy there? All kinds of things ran through my mind. I dared not call him back. I made it to my place and called Paisley.

She did not answer. I took off my church clothes and put on my night clothes. He still did not come. I called Anthony and no answer. After waiting for over an hour, Paisley called and stated, "I was wondering what was happening?"

"With what?"

"Anthony said he had just arrived and I hadn't heard anything else."

"I called you and you didn't answer either."

"I was busy."

"Busy doing what?"

"My man was here, Ainsley," my sister said rudely.

"Oh."

"Oh what?"

"Did he get the boys?"

"No. I told him I would keep them while y'all

talk."

"Ok. Thanks, Paisley. What about your car?"

"I can get it later and you're welcome."

I got off the phone and Anthony knocked on the door. I didn't speak. I just stood there when he opened the door to ask, "What is it?"

"I had been talking to Paisley and—"

He stopped me and said, "Let us not use this moment to chat about your sister." He tried kissing me, but I turned my head away. He moved back and looked at me funny. "What's wrong?"

"I don't feel well. I think you need to go."

"What?" he surprisingly asked, for I have never denied him.

"Anthony, I don't feel good."

The truth is him being here did not feel right anymore. I downplayed him and the attention he was trying to give me. Then my body caught hold of my mind. This body of mine became dizzy as well as warm. My love said, "You feel warm. You need to lie down, or go to the doctor."

"No, I will be ok."

Chapter 12

I woke up looking at a strange ceiling. Anthony was by my side as I asked, "Where am I? What happened?"

"You passed out on me, and I didn't know what to do."

"Where am I?"

"You in the hospital."

"Where my boys?"

"They still with your sister."

"Ok. What they say wrong with me?"

"They haven't said anything yet."

The young nurse with an hourglass shape came in and spoke, "Mrs. Vaughn?"

I glanced at her and said, "I am Ms. Rudolph."

"Oh, I am sorry. When he signed his name, I guess the hospital automatically assumed you were his wife."

"What is wrong with me?"

"Do you want to talk in front of him?"

My senses became keen as I heard those

words. He glanced at me, and I didn't want him to hear whatever it was, but I knew he wanted to hear it. I said, "Yeah, he is my fiancé. You can talk in front of him."

"You were pregnant in your tubes."

"What? I can't have kids. My tubes are tied, and I don't have a uterus."

"You have a uterus. Well, had a uterus and your tubes weren't tied. They were slightly clamped."

"Clamped? Wait, I had a uterus? I wasn't tied? What are you saying?"

"You were pregnant in your tubes, which resulted in a tubal pregnancy. The baby planted itself in your tubes."

I was shocked. "I had this surgery years ago. The doctor told me my tubes were tied and if I'm not mistaken my uterus was taken out. There is no way I was pregnant,"

"You might need to take that up with whoever performed the surgery you are talking about."

"Is my baby ok?"

She stared at me in a blank way. Anthony said, "Ley, the baby is gone."

I wanted to cry. I finally got the baby I wanted Paisley to carry, and I ended up carrying it myself. I loudly asked with a question on my heart, "How far along was I?"

"Almost eight weeks but your diabetes became part of the problem but not the complete problem. You were on the brink of death when he brought you in here. Your life was being threatened. As for the child, it would never be born alive."

The look on my face caused Anthony to touch my hand and say, "It'll be ok."

I looked at the nurse and asked, "Will I be able to carry another child?"

"No. He had to do a salpingectomy."

The tears no longer stayed in my eyes. They found their way out my eyes and onto my cheeks. Bowing my head and letting it all out, I sobbed nonstop. I heard the nurse say to Anthony, "I will leave you both alone."

She left out and I held my head up. Anthony handed me a towel and I kept crying. I've been trying to get a baby by the man I loved and the baby slipped between my grasp. Nothing else mattered. Not even my sons, who are already here. I only thought of me and my baby by Anthony. I was supposed to have the perfect family. My love didn't have any children and I was the first to carry his seed.

I cried. The thought of losing his seed saddened me. Anthony said, "Cheer up. You will be happy as the day goes on."

"I can't. I lost our only chance at happiness. I was to make you a father."

He did not respond as Paisley walked in the door. He got up and greeted her. She smiled as he stated under his breath, "You look nice today."

"Thank you. How is Ainsley?"

"She is awake and crying," he spoke as he looked at Paisley.

Paisley looked at me and sat down to say, "The boys are in the waiting room with my man."

"They don't know I am here, do they?"

"No. I didn't tell them."

"Thank you."

"Excuse me, ladies, for a sec."

When Anthony closed the door Paisley asked silently, "What was wrong?"

I started crying. She sat on the edge of the bed and gave me a hug. Her hug felt cold and untrue. I forgot all about it and cried, "I lost my baby."

"You were pregnant?" she asked with surprise.

"Yes. I was pregnant and had a salpingectomy because the baby attached itself in my tubes. I didn't know I was clamped. I thought my tubes were tied and wasn't sure about my uterus."

"Oh, Ainsley. I am so sorry," my sister said.

"I know. Now my chance to have a child by him is over."

"Not quite."

"Huh?"

"I got pregnant."

"It worked?" I asked as I glanced up at her.

"Yes, you can say it worked."

"You having a baby."

"I am having you and Anthony's baby."

"Really?"

"Yes. I am pregnant."

"You will give the baby to me?"

"Yes! It was your idea and I'm not married, nor do I want a baby right now."

I started crying, this time tears of joy. I asked, "Anthony know?"

"Yes, he knows."

"You told him first."

"I had gotten sick. That was why it took him so long to come over. He went out and got me a test. He was there when I took it, and he was so thrilled. Those two pink lines showed up. He asked me if it was his, because you told him about what we did. I told him it was, and he asked about his homeboy getting it. I told him he doesn't have to worry about it."

"That's why you couldn't answer your phone, when I kept calling you and him."

"I fell out before you did. After Anthony came to your house, you fell out. I guess it's a twin thing," she said with joy.

She smiled as she said, "Anthony was not mad. My man, now that is another story."

"He knows its Anthony's baby?"

"I am breaking up with him, so he won't know. Plus, he has never slept with me, and can't possibly think it is his baby."

"No chance, at all?"

"Hell no!"

A snicker came out my mouth as she stated, "We been together for a few months and really don't want him."

"Why he still hanging around?"

"He thinks I will change my mind, but I have something better than him."

"A new man, perhaps?"

"Not quite. But today is not the day we discuss me. It's about you."

Anthony came back in smiling. I asked, "Why didn't you tell me?"

"I thought since it was your idea to include her, she should be the one to tell you."

Paisley stood up and Anthony told her, "I will come by and bring you some fruits."

I thought about the strawberries I had that night with him. Paisley said, "I go back to the doctor next week to hear the heartbeat and see pictures. You going?"

"Yes!" I screamed.

Anthony shouted, "Me too."
I added, "You may come, since it is your child."

He smiled and gave Paisley a hug. She left and I asked, "Why the change of heart?"

"What you mean?"

"You got mad and said I better hope it didn't work."

"I went to see Paisley that night. We talked and I feel her. I understand. She persuaded me into thinking about children. She was good and I fell for it."

"You not mad."

"Nope."

"You tell Hadley?"

"I told her I was done with you and her."

"What?"

"I had to let her think I was done with you and her, so she would not be hounding you about shit."

"Oh. What you think about the baby?"

"I am more excited than I thought I would be."

"You are about to be a dad."

"I know. You don't get that every day."

"I know. I am glad you got her to do it."

"Well, we share the same DNA. The baby would be like me as well, as if I had it myself."

"I am going to make sure she takes care of herself."

"Thank you."

"You get well. I'm about to go."

"Go where?"

"Back to my house."

I was trying to think of something to keep him, so I asked, "What Hadley ever say about getting hit or choking me?"

"She never said a word about it. We didn't talk about it. It's one of those things we put under the rug and leave it there."

"Oh."

He leaned over and gave me a peck on the forehead. It was different. I said, "Is that new cologne?"

"Yes. You like it?"

"I do."

"Get well."

He left and I dozed off. I know it was about an hour or two before the doctor came in. He was a tall man with dark-brown hair said, "My nurse told me she has spoken with you. Do you have any questions?"

"Yes. She said I had a salpingectomy. What did you take out?"

"The baby was in the right tube, and I had taken that out. Your left tube was severely damaged from bad abortions, so I took that out as well."

"Will I be able to get pregnant?"

"Man speaking, no, but God can do anything."

"Ok. When will I go home?"

"You can go home sometime tomorrow evening."

He left out and I just lay there, unable to think. I called Anthony and he did not answer. I called Paisley and she didn't answer at first. When she did, she was laughing, I had to ask, "What is so funny?"

"Anthony just came over and he's being silly."

The only thing I heard was he came over. I questioned dryly, "He did."

"He said he has to make sure I eat and get plenty of rest."

"That was hours ago."

"And?"

"And he is my man" I reminded my sister.

"I am not after him. I am carrying his baby. I guess he wants to make sure I am ok. You in the hospital and can't check on me. You know all this is new and I have a lot of emotions. There is a baby growing inside of me; that is the result of your idea."

"I'm sorry."

"It's okay. You just being protective and think of the way you got him."

I was quiet and she was right. To change the subject, I added, "Well, I get out tomorrow. If you don't mind, put him on the phone."

The next tone I heard was a dark one, saying, "What's up?"

"Why you not answering my phone call?"

"Hadley was with me, so I had to leave. I made an excuse and she bought it."

"Oh."

"When will you be able to come home?"

"Sometime tomorrow evening. Can you come and get me?"

"I can. What time?"

"Be here by six, I guess."

"I'll be there for you."

"What time you leaving from Paisley's?"

"I don't know. Why?"

"I'm just asking. I can't ask?"

"You can ask what you want. It doesn't mean I have to answer."

I didn't like that, even if it is true. I asked, "What you mean?"

"You aren't my wife and if I don't want to answer you, I don't have too."

He has never talked like that to me. Lately he has been acting weird. I decided to get an attitude back by saying, "I am your woman. I am the second woman in your life and if I want to ask questions, I expect you to answer."

"Yeah, I am sorry. You are the main woman I love. I guess I was thinking how I would have had two children at once. It kind of hurt me too, Ley, but I know God knows best. With that in mind, I am not sad anymore."

"That sounds better."

"Get some rest and I will see you in the morning."

"Tell Paisley I will talk to her later. Good night. I love you."

"Love you too, Ley."

Chapter 13

All through the night, I could not sleep. My thoughts were on Paisley and Anthony. *I hope they aren't sleeping together or trying too. I already have Hadley as competition; I don't need another bitch playing.* That idea made me very angry. Ever since, I told him about my sister carrying our baby, they had been acting funny. I quit thinking about my man and my sister because my head started hurting. I closed my eyes and the air seemed thick when they were here.

Then again, I could be acting this way because I lost my baby, and she is still carrying hers. Although, the doctor says no, I must get pregnant again and quickly as possible.

I am glad Hadley isn't trying to get pregnant; that would complicate everything. I really pray that bitch stay where she at. She needs to give him the divorce and quit holding onto a man who doesn't want or desire her. Why am I thinking of these things, after the message I heard at the revival? Oddly enough, my baby died, and it could have been a sign for me. I should be walking away but how can I, when I have a lot invested? That is probably why Hadley feels the same way. She has invested a little more than I because they are still legally married.

Anthony did say I can't make him do anything he doesn't want too. He says if he wanted his wife, he would be with her and faithful no doubt. My love has told me he loves me and won't hurt her. It hit me. He is right. I can't make him, or any man, do anything they don't want. If Hadley was doing her job I never would have been in the picture. It's her fault.

Everything is her fault and not mine. I am sure he has reached out to her about their loveless marriage. I am glad she sucks at being a wife for my man. Now is the time for demonstrating how important I am in his life. Anthony will still see me as the wife material he has said I am I closed my eyes at those thoughts and finally went to sleep.

I must have slept all day. I awoke to the evening and saw my diabetic medicine. I took it and saw old women pushing carts with arts, crafts and books. Old hags, I thought while rolling my eyes and head. I didn't want anything but to go home. One of them saw me. Her look told me she read my thoughts. As she was coming over, I quickly turned my head. She tapped my leg and said, "Would you like some crafts? Young lady would you like some artwork or perhaps a book to read?"

"No," I stated without looking at her.

"You must be going home today, young lady."

"I am," I responded flatly.

She continued to stand there. I faced her and said disgustedly, "Do you mind? I am trying to rest."

The old lady tilted her head. She glared in my face saying, "Honey, there is no rest for the wicked."

I was caught off guard as I asked, "What you say?"

The other two women walked out the door. She said it again, but with more force. "There is no rest for the wicked. You don't need to just go home. You really need to repent. My spirit tells me you are not truly godly sorrow for your evil deeds. You will pay if you don't stop it."

"How you going to tell me how I feel? I know what I am sorry for and what I am not."

"You hide really well, but you can't fool me. You are wicked and you will have your part in the lake of fire."

"Lake of fire," I mocked and laughed at her.

The old lady said, "Your flesh has gotten you in trouble this day."

"Get on out my room and take your damn curses with you."

"I will go, but you are going to wish you had listened. Mark my words, what I tell you is not a curse but a fact."

She left out and I didn't give her another thought. I am waiting to see my love. A young nurse from earlier came in. She seems young and naïve. The girl took out my IV and told me she will be back. I waited another thirty minutes and still no

Anthony. I called him again. This time I heard a woman's voice say, "Hey, girl. You feel better today?" It was Paisley.

A question crossed my face. I've never answered his phone and I am wondering what is happening, so I asked, "Why are you answering Anthony's phone?"

"He told me to answer it because he is letting Jared swing the bat."

"He stayed the night?" I asked with a small attitude.

"No. He came by to see if I wanted a ride to the hospital," she responded with an attitude.

"Well. I was waiting on him and for you to answer his phone sounds like some shit to me."

Ignoring me, she yelled, "Its Ainsley."

"Tell her I'm coming."

"I heard him," I said to her before she could tell me what he said.

"Ainsley, why you acting funny? I don't want your dick."

"How am I acting funny? You and Anthony act

like y'all are best friends but before, y'all didn't talk much. Hell, I don't answer his phone then you answer it. So yeah, I'm curious."

"Well, I am having his baby for y'all. This is yawl's baby, remember? He wants to be involved. The truth is he comes to see your boys and be a father to them more than anything. All the time he is here, he is with them until they fall asleep. You already share him with a wife. What do I look like going behind my twin, who is already going behind somebody else's back?"

"Well, just tell him to come on."

"Okay."

"You coming too?"

"No. I am going to stay home with the boys. I was throwing up and sick like crazy."

I felt saddened because it should be me with the morning sickness, but I got over it. "Eat some saltine crackers and drink some Sprite."

"I've done that, and it did not work. I feel better and I think this little embryo knows the dad because when he came over, I felt better."

"When is your next appointment?" I asked to shut her up about my man.

"Next week. I don't know the time."

"I am going to come with you."

"You want me to bring them over today, when you get home?"

"Yeah, you can for a little while."

"Okay, and send me some clothes by him."

"You need anything else?"

"No, just some clothes."

We got off the phone. If I know my twin, she is going to send a comb, deodorant and other items. I got up and took a bath. When I came out, the nurse was in my room. She was talking to Anthony. He smiled and she laughed. He saw me and the look on my face and said, "Baby, here your clothes."

She turned and saw me and said, "Ms. Rudolph, when you get dressed, I'll be back with your instructions."

The nurse looked at my man and left out with a smile. I asked, "What the hell was that all about?"

"What you mean?"

"What were y'all talking about?"

"Nothing. I told her she reminded me of a cousin of mine."

"Really?"

"Yeah. It wasn't shit worth talking about. I told her I am married."

"Married to whom?"

"Her for now, but you in the future so come here, girl."

He pulled me close and said, "I love you, Ainsley. Stop acting like every woman is a threat, when they are not."

I started getting dressed and saw all the other things my sister packed. I smiled because I know my sister, because I know me. I am wrong for the things I had been thinking. If it were anything I would know it. To make sure my thoughts are correct, I asked nicely with no clue or suspicion of them by saying, "You have been spending time over there."

"I mainly have been with our boys."

"Our boys, huh?"

"Yes. Jared and Kyle are our boys. I love them just as much as you do. I treat them as a father does his children. Hurry up and get ready while I go get the nurse."

"You don't have to go get her. I can buzz her."

I reached for the hospital call and told the front desk I was ready. She came in with a wheelchair. I watched how she acted. She explained my instructions. Anthony kept his head turned. She didn't look at him either. She left and he asked, "You ready."

"Yeah."

I got in the wheelchair and Anthony pushed me out as the nurse walked with us. I felt like they were lip syncing behind my back. I got up and got in the front seat. She took the wheelchair and smiled as she left. He got in and we drove off. I said, "You staying tonight with me? I need you."

"We'll see," was all he said as he drove. I reached over and touched his hand. He gave it a squeeze. I leaned on his shoulder, and he kept driving. He must have forgotten I was in the car because he drove me by his house. I saw Hadley's Audi. It had the trunk up. He sped up soon as I looked at him. I asked, "Hadley back at home?"

"No."

"Well why was the trunk up on the Audi?"

"I had that up. I plan on cleaning it out."

"Don't you want to go let the trunk down?"

"You are more important than that car."

I did not say another word because the words he spoke did not set well. He acted like it was nothing to let the trunk stay up on a hundred-thousand-dollar car. My gut tells me he lying, but I know he is married, so why would he lie? He doesn't have a reason to. But for some reason he is not honest with me. As we pulled up to my apartment I stated calmly, "If she is there, tell me. You don't have to lie. Be real with me. That is how we have always been."

He did not look at me as he got out and opened the door for me. He helped me walk to my front door. He opened the door and to my surprise, Paisley and the boys were there. My loves ran to me happily. I was overjoyed. She had a cake, and the apartment was decorated. I cried. He came over and spoke, "I got you off guard with the trunk up on the car. Did it work?"

"Yes, it did."

We kissed. At that moment, I felt complete. Everyone I ever cared about was with me. Paisley walked over and said, "You and your suspicions."

"I know," I answered, ashamed of my thoughts of her and him.

"I couldn't tell you. It was his idea and I rolled with it. He stayed all night getting this together."

I looked and didn't see anything that possibly took all night. She saw my eyes and spoke happily, "It is more than what you think it looks like."

Ignoring her, I played with my boys. For a long while, I had so much fun. Me losing my baby did not bother me as much. I felt sad because I was so obsessed with having Anthony's child that my boys were robbed of my attention and affection. My thoughts were of my man and my sister, until I heard Paisley say, "It is not moving yet."

Anthony was touching her stomach. I didn't like it. I'm beginning to think it was a bad idea for her to carry the baby for us, although she is my sister, and it was her egg. Anthony disturbed me by saying, "I'm about to take Paisley and the boys home before I go home."

My boys were whining. They did not want to go to bed. I was a bit angry because now those two must be alone. I know from experience it doesn't take long for sex or get a nut. Paisley took the boys to their room. Anthony said, "I'm just dropping her off and going home. I am tired. I had a long night."

"Doing what?"

"Planning this for you."

"It didn't take long for this."

"I had to go find the stuff we did get. Put it up and get rest."

"I'm sorry," I spoke to stop the argument.

"I will call you when I get home. If I forget

call me."

"Okay. I love you so much, Anthony."

"I love you too, Ainsley."

Paisley entered the room and said, "The boys are sleep. You ready to take me home? I am tired."

"Yeah," Anthony spoke as she gave me a hug.

She walked out the door and he was watching the sway of her hips. He saw me watching and started laughing. Anthony walked out the door and I locked it. I peeped out the window and he was in the car pulling off. My mind was in the car with them, wondering what the conversations were about. I waited until I thought; he should be at home and called. Paisley answered his phone. I asked, "Where is Anthony?"

"He left his phone."

"Oh."

"Ainsley, you don't have any worry on my end. I am your sister, and he is not my type. Quit wondering about me with your man. He is your man, and you are my sister."

"I know. I am just cautious that's all."

"You have every right to be cautious. Get some rest and I will get the boys in the morning."

"Okay. Good night."

I could not sleep. I was being tortured with my mind about my man and my sister. In my dreams, I saw them in the bed together making good love. I would get up and think. I would pace the floor. This must be how Hadley felt when her husband would be out. Times like this, I need a car. When did Paisley come get her car? Why come she didn't drive her car here, instead of Anthony driving her home? I thought as my mind would not leave me alone. I decided on calling him. When I did, a sleepy woman's voice spoke, "Hello."

I did not say a word, but my mind was questioning who it was. I did not catch the voice. The woman said, "I know you're not calling my husband's phone in the middle of the night." I hung up. I thought Paisley said he left his phone. I checked the time, and it was four in the morning. Now I'm wondering is Hadley sleeping with

Anthony. What she doing at his house? Where is he at? When did he get his phone from Paisley's? What's really going on? If Paisley had never taken her car, I would've driven by his house to see if there was another car there. Realizing I could not do anything about it, I went to bed angry, miserable and full of questions.

Chapter 14

During the night, I had a wet dream about my man. I hadn't had his dick in a while, and I was feeling it now. My pussy throbbed and reminded me of the loneliness it has been in. The drought has been serious. Now I will be sleeping with him for a mission. At first, it was plain sex and then I got pregnant by the grace of God, only to lose it. I sighed and got up. I took a shower and started cooking breakfast as my boys slept.

When I finished, I gave them a bath and fixed their plates. My sons sat down to eat. They both were being talkative among themselves as I was enjoying the communication. My sons had never talked so much before until today and I don't know what gives. Between nibbles of food, my son Jared said as he ate, "Uncle Anthony would put us to bed and in the morning cook breakfast just like this, Momma."

I nearly choked when I heard him, but I didn't think I heard it right. My son kept eating as if he did not say anything wrong. I gathered my words and asked nicely, "What you say, Jared?"

"TT Paisley said he Uncle Anthony. He put us to bed at night then he cooks breakfast in the morning. His eggs are better than yours. Momma but yours is good too, Momma."

"Cooking eggs," I spoke, hiding my true feelings. "These good. Ain't they, Kyle?"

My baby boy only nodded his head as he ate. I got up and went in my room and fell on the floor weeping soundlessly. I did not try to think or figure out what he is doing at my sister's house early in the morning. Jared came in my room and said, "Uncle Anthony on the phone."

He handed me the phone and went back in the kitchen. I didn't respond right away. I hung it up. He called back and I answered above a whisper, "Hello."

"Ainsley, this you?"

"Who else you hoped it to be?"

"Just you. I want to know did you call me early this morning?"

"Yes. You told me to call you if you didn't call me. I waited long as I could. When I awoke, you were on my mind. Why?"

"I left my phone at your sister's. She brought it over. After she left, I woke up and Hadley was there picking up items. She told me you called, and she asked you why you are calling this time of morning. She said you need to respect her house. But I told her that's my phone and my private life."

"Why does she answer your phone? I don't even answer your phone."

"She normally doesn't, and she is still my wife."

"The boys told me they are calling you Uncle Anthony."

"That is your sister's idea," he said as if he were smiling.

I did not question him about anything else. I hung up on him and he kept calling back. I came out the room and got the boys. I left my phone on purpose as we walked to the neighborhood park. They were having so much fun. I see now my sole purpose is to be a better mother to my boys and not get sidetracked again. We stayed for almost three hours. We walked back home, and they took a bath. I put on some cartoons as I boiled hot dogs, and prepared apple slices, along with potato chips and Berry Blend V-8 juice.

They came in the kitchen and sat down as I fixed their plates. I ate the apple slices as they ate the rest of the food. I did my best not to question my sons, but I asked as I took my medicine, "You guys like Uncle Anthony playing baseball with you?"

"I like him a lot, but I think TT Paisley likes him a lot too," Jared added.

"How so?"

"She always smiles when he comes over. He even kissed her on the hair."

"On the hair," I stated as I hid the hurt on my face.

Jared used his hand and touched the top of his head. I smiled and laughed. He said, "He is with us all the time."

"He does."

"You at home and we at TT Paisley house. They always hugging and playing around. They have a lot of fun."

"They do?"

"Yes. At night, we can hear her playing with him. Calling him, but I thought he left."

"What you do?" I had to ask.

"I go back to sleep."

My nerves shook every ounce of blood in me. I did not gather my emotional thoughts. They were all over the place. How long they have been creeping, is the question? How long have I been looking like a fool thinking Hadley was my problem? Is she in love? Is he in love? Did it really work, or did they have sex for it to work? Does Hadley know he's cheating on us? A silent tear slipped down my cheek. I removed myself from the table and went in the living room. I thought what if your son is wrong? Think of all you have been through with him; why would he hurt you?

I could not answer any questions. If someone would have put this treachery in a movie featuring my life; I would not have believed it even if I saw it. I don't believe the two people I love are fooling around. What if I am wrong? What if Jared misunderstood it all because he doesn't know what he is really seeing, I thought as I sat there. Somehow, I could see her enjoying the love from the man I love. I could see Paisley making him feel just as good as I make him. I can't let another woman come between him and me, sister or not.

I love my dear sis, but I love my man more, because he has always been there for me. Anthony understood me when I didn't have anyone. I closed my eyes and recalled from nowhere, warning comes before destruction. Remember God sends his men and women to warn people of their ways, their sin. Many times, the people don't listen. Instead, they do what they want even after they were warned. The world does not understand how the things of this world can turn their heart from God. Greed and lust comes in and takes over.

The people don't know how to prioritize because they have lost their passion for God and have a more sinful lifestyle. "All the people answered, 'HIS blood is on us and on our children.' I know this means if I am not teaching my children how to live for the Lord, they will learn of my sinful behavior. They won't know how to live for Christ because they have not been taught. Are you heeding the warning that has come your way? Do you still play the victim when you really aren't? Those two alone starts the downfall of man who loves the things of this world rather than the things of God.

I opened my eyes and quit thinking. My head was aching. I went in the bathroom and got an aspirin and a sip of water. I heard my cell phone ring. Kyle took off and got it out my room. It was a text from Anthony.

Anthony: Please come over with the boys. We need to talk.

I replied: How?

Anthony: Paisley.

I did not respond. I sat the phone down and Paisley called. I didn't want to answer but I don't want her to be suspicious; just yet. I answered, "Greetings, my twin."

She laughed and said, "I hadn't heard that in a while."

"I know. What's going on?" I spoke to hide my anger.

"Anthony wants me to bring you to his house in a little while. You ok with that?"

"When are you coming so we will be ready?"

"He told me about eight."

"Okay. We will be ready."

"Where is he at?" I asked.

"I don't know. He text me that, and I text you that."

All day I tried clearing my mind about my circumstance. My sons were happy and to see them smiling and being happy children meant the world to me. When I needed family love and support, she did not give it. I was alone until Anthony came and showed me real love. His name made my head ache. My son Kyle was crying and saying, "Mommy, I don't die."

"You can't go anywhere until Jesus says so, but what are you talking about?"

"Jared said we gone die.'

I yelled at Jared to come here and he did. I asked, "Why you say that?"

He looked at me and said, "When we do stuff wrong; that's what happen."

"Where those come from?"

He shrugged his shoulders and I scolded, "Don't make your brother afraid."

"But, Mom."

"Don't 'but Mom' me. Don't tell your brother things like that. He is too young to think about death. You both are young children and I want you to enjoy life as children."

"Okay."

"Now give him a hug and tell him you love him."

Jared obeyed and I said, "Now come here. It's a group hug."

They started laughing as I did. My boys started back playing again. I watched them play and smile for another hour. They both told me they love me, and I said, "There is nothing I wouldn't do for you both and my love for you is undying. Do you hear me?"

"Yes," Kyle said but Jared said, "Momma, I want a new home. Can we get a home up there?"

"Up where?"

He pointed to the sky. I smiled and said, "Yes. Our spiritual home is in the sky, but our earthly home is in a new place. You may be right. We might need to leave this place and start over. So much has gone on here and a fresh start might be what we all need."

"TT Paisley coming?" Jared asked.

"I don't know we will have to ask her and see."

Instantly, I thought of just leaving Anthony and Paisley. Finding my own man and leaving all this alone. The idea of leaving this area sounding good and I liked it. My son said, "Mommy, I am sleepy."

I saw Kyle wiping his eyes and then Paisley blew her horn. I looked at my cell and saw it was indeed eight. I said, "Get your bags. We are going to Uncle Anthony's."

Their demeanor perked up happier than ever as they dashed off for their bags. I stuck my head out the door and said, "We coming."

The boys came out and I locked the door. To some degree, something did not feel right. I was going to stay but the boys ran towards her car. I followed their lead. I got in the car and as I was buckling down Paisley said, "You good?"

"Good about what?" I asked her without looking at her directly.

"You don't look so happy."

"Oh, I am. I am just learning some things," I spoke briefly.

"What are you learning, my dear sister?" Paisley teased.

"How to be quiet and how to leave other people's things alone," I responded nicely.

She was quiet as she said, "What you got up your sleeve?"

"Nothing. What you got up yours?" I questioned back in a sly tease.

"Nothing but having this baby and giving it to its proper owners."

I smiled and looked at her stomach with happiness. It wasn't as flat as it used to look. I know she is being attached to the little one and I don't blame her. I spoke truthfully, "I know you love with all your heart, my sis, and I do love you no matter how I feel about things."

"You okay, Ainsley? You seem distant from me, I guess. I haven't done anything to you, have I?"

"Yeah, been thinking and having an eye-opening experience. You know, I am thankful for all the lessons people have taught me in my life. I've learned a lot from them when I didn't understand my life. But I am getting it now." Remembering her question, I asked nice and oblivious, "Have you done something to me that I don't know about?"

"No. I have always been on your side and done

nothing but helping you. Ainsley, you are my family. I trust you know I would never hurt you on purpose. I feel I would be able to talk to you about anything; good or bad. You have been more than a twin. You have been my best friend and it's because of you I am experiencing this joy. Thank you for letting me in on your life," Paisley added with love.

"You're welcome, twin."

She didn't say another word as she drove. The boys were happy as they looked out the windows. I asked curiously, "What does Anthony want, anyway?"

"I really don't know."

"It must be important for him to call us over this time of night."

"I don't know. He normally calls but this time he texts me," Paisley spoke.

"Hadley must be in the picture," I asked.

"I doubt she is," my twin casually spoke.

"What makes you think she is not?"

"I'm just saying she is his wife, whether we like her or not. They aren't divorced," Paisley just had to add.

"True, but she did leave him, remember?"

"What if he put her out and claimed she left? What if he is really lying to you like he was to her?"

"What are you getting at?" I asked her harshly.

"I don't have a problem with her, as long as she's out the picture for you. That makes me glad. You being happy are the foremost thing on my mind and if having this baby would not bring you happiness, I would not do it. But I know you would do the same for me if I were in your shoes. You have always helped me. I never understood how you love until now. I guess I was always in your shadow and now I am in my own light," my sister said in a convincing way.

"Is there anything I should know?"

"I don't have anything to tell you and I don't know of anything you should know. You have always been the smart twin and you know it all," I heard my sister say.

"No, I don't. I make mistakes and learn from them. I wish I knew it all" I spoke with humor.

"I have always admired you and how you live."

"How is that? I have been the black sheep of the family. Mom and Dad were horrible to me. You know what was done to me as a child, don't you?"

"Yes," she spoke slowly as if she didn't want to say anything.

"Why you say it like that?" I wondered as I asked her that question.

"It's a sore spot for you and we don't need to talk about anything that will make you feel sad."

"It is. I can't change what happened. I don't want my children to go through what I went through, that's why I want them to grow up to be respectful young men."

"You have done a great job," she said with admiration.

We were quiet. Then, I said, "I guess that is why I fell for Anthony so hard and so fast."

"How is that? He is thoughtful. He knows how to make you feel better about what you have going on in your life, in spite of what he may have going on in his life. You would never know the pain he may be feeling, because he hides it well. Overall, he is a likable kind of guy."

"I guess I overlooked the fact he could have been married or in some type of relationship, because I was about to kill myself and the two I love. Anthony changed it. He gave me reasons to live and to love. He challenged me and allowed me to love me again, when I hadn't for a long time. Men used me and I used me. I didn't know I could have a real emotional bond with a man who could make he believe in me, believe in love again. You know what I'm saying, Paisley?"

"Wow. I didn't know you were about to kill you all, Ainsley. I'm glad you met him and thankful he has made you love again."

"Yes. Anthony showed me the love I have needed, when I needed it. At first, he was just someone I knew as a friend. Over time, it grew into something more, because we allowed it. I could have removed myself from his life when his wife told me to get out if their marriage, but I couldn't. I wouldn't. I was too far gone and seeing him or talking to him when I could meant holding on that we may be together like we are now. I get him. I understand Anthony in more ways than I should have. I don't know what I would've done if he had left me alone completely."

Giving me a smile and a light hand squeeze, Paisley spoke "Anthony has a way of making you see true potential and he always tells you the truth and that makes him a great guy. Not trying to toot his horn, but I don't see how being married to his wife could've gone wrong. I can't imagine him hurting her or you."

"You talk of him not hurting me. I couldn't imagine him being married, because of all the time we spent together and all the phone conversations we had."

We were quiet as I sighed, "Oh, Paisley. I wish things had been different I wish he had met me before he married her. My life would be the best right now."

"Or maybe, he could've met and married you and cheat on you like he is doing her. For her to be so bad and he still stayed with her, tells a lot about his character, to be honest. However, there are two sides to every coin. Too bad we only heard his side."

"That's all in the past. She left him and I am here to pick up his broken pieces. Sure, after I was in the relationship knee deep, I found out he was married. By then it was too late. I couldn't un-love him as I should have. That's why I made it my business to love him as a wife loves her husband. But what do you do when you find the man who makes you feel like you are the one?"

"You pray he is honest with his feelings and not playing games."

She drove for a few more moments and we arrived. The trunk was still up on the Audi and I asked, "Why is the trunk still up?"

"I don't know. He told me he was going to clean it out."

"He told me that too" I confirmed to Paisley.

Paisley got out and said, "I will take the boys around back to the swing set Anthony had bought."

"I didn't know he bought a swing set for them," I uttered while wondering how she knew more than I do.

"Yeah. He bought it for them a few days ago. He says he wants them to experience being young boys and having fun."

"Okay, I agree with that," I spoke as I went to the front of the house. I did not knock. I walked right in. The house was dark, but I know he is here. His car is parked outside, but no him. I turned around and that was all I remembered.

Chapter 15

I felt groggy as I moaned a little. The icy water hit me. I heard, "Wake your thirsty ass up. You should have drunk water and not my husband's nut."

I could not scream loud because of the huge piece of gray tape on my mouth. The voice said, "You going to learn what it means to keep your mouth shut and off my dick."

It was Hadley's voice. When I became fully aware, I saw her. She had on a white doctor's coat and a matching scrub outfit. I looked around and noticed I was in her bedroom, naked and all tied up like a sexual display from the chains I saw the first time I was there. I could see Anthony asleep, gagged, but naked. She even has him hog tied to the bed from both ends. I wondered where my boys are. Tilting my head some, I saw my sons. Each one of them was laying on the floor on a pallet sleep. I looked around for Paisley. My eyes found hers. She was tied and gag to a chair. Hadley spread her arms wide and cheerfully announced, "I am glad the gang's all here," before leaving out the room.

I tried jerking the chains for freedom, but nothing happened. Moments later she returned with a huge chef's pot. She came near me to say as if we were in a conversation, "Let me start with my husband. I'm sure Anthony has told you that I have never been a cook but today, I'm cooking that ass!

Wake up, Anthony!"

Hadley slowly emptied scalding hot water
all onto his naked body. He started shaking and
trying to jerk his arms from the posts. He screamed,
but all I heard was a whimper because his mouth
was still covered. She left out and returned again
and emptied another pot of scalding hot water on
him, slower than she did the first time. The once
erotic skin on my man became a shedding egg white
color as the flesh fell from his muscles.
He closed his eyes. I assumed he passed out from
all the pain and shock of her dousing the water on
him. The broiler made a loud thumping sound as
she threw it on the floor. She looked at Anthony and
then to the rest of us and spoke, "Now let me have
the field since you all played in the game."

I am terrified at what she just done to the man
she claims to love. His wife walked towards me. I
tried begging and crying through the tape, to make
sure she heard, "Please don't hurt my children.
They are innocent."

She heard me and gave a devious smile
directly in my painful face. She placed her right
hand over her heart with the left hand on top. Her
heartless words were, "Oh sweet Ainsley. No one in
this room is innocent."

I could see the evil in her eyes, and it tore at
me. She walks over to my sleeping son Jared. My
heart is fluttering as she spoke, "You mean this little

bastard that hit me with a bat. You mean he is innocent? No, not him. He just can't be innocent just because you said so."

As loud as I could, I begged her. My heart froze. Hadley removed a gun with a silencer from her doctor's coat. She went on and said, "Your children are a part of you and any part of you must die. I am getting rid of a generation of vipers that won't hurt anyone else. There is no way I can live and let that happen, toodles."

Giving me a final smile, she fatally shot my son at point blank range twice in the back of the head. She looked at me having no sympathy whatsoever. Hadley stood over Kyle and said, "If I let this one live, he would come after me because of what I did to that bat swinging bastard brother of his. Could that happen? Nah. I can't let that happen. Unlike you, I have to clean up my past. Say goodbye."

This monster shot my other son three times in the face. Blood was splattering everywhere. I was bucking and bucking trying to get loose but couldn't. She said, "You and your personal agenda involved your children. If you had stayed out the way, none of this would have happened so shut up and blame yourself. I told you to stay away."

I was just hanging there wishing she had killed me and not my babies. How could a demon so full of hate kill children? As if she read my mind, she said, "Children are not innocent. When he hit me, he got more involved in this matter, than he already was. Sure, he didn't know his precious mother is a deceitful, cunning, vengeful, manipulative, bitter and wicked bitch; among other adjectives. But in your mind, I'm the beast. Grow up. He and his little brother had no idea how you were breaking up my home with your ways but that's neither here nor there. They both are dead. End of the story."

Hadley walked over to my sister and said, "Now this bitch right here. She deserves a fate worse than death. If I could kill her, wake her back up and kill her again, I would. Once for you; once for me. But once you're dead, you're dead. Believe me, she deserves to be killed, twice and that's nice."

Hadley hit Paisley with the end of the gun. Paisley woke some but was out of it. Anthony's wife said, "She partook in the sins of her sister and my husband. That makes her guilty as sin. I know so much because I had my faithful husband followed. Ainsley, when you thought you were fucking my world up, he was fucking your world up by fucking the hell out of your dear beloved twin sister. She was getting more dick than you were."

I gasped and she said, "What, you didn't know?"

Tears flowed from me. She walked over to me and yanked the tape off. I yelled at Anthony, "I ought to cut your dick off and put it in an ant bed of red ants, you dickless son of a bitch!"

"Ooh, but it was ok for you to be screwing the dickless son of a bitch behind my back. You weren't trying to put the dick in an ant bed then. I don't want to hear that."

She let me speak; therefore, I spoke with little life I had left, "I tried telling you I was sorry. He wouldn't let me talk to you."

"Keep your damn apologies. Even if he didn't tell you, I told you when you first came in our lives to leave. You weren't satisfied until you had him and now sin has you and your family involved in my marriage. When people are married you don't get in it. I told you, I told you, I told you, I told you. You wouldn't listen. I already knew what I was going to do if I caught him AGAIN. You just didn't know. Now you will know. When I heard the man in the park, telling you about you, I almost had a heart until you kept at my husband."

She walked back to Paisley and took off her tape. My sister stared at me and said, "I am so sorry for hurting you. I fell for him. He wooed me and made me believe the world. Especially when we found out—"

Hadley cut her off. Mocking Paisley, Hadley said, "You naïve ass. You are her twin. How could you screw behind your sister's back? Now my back is one thing, but hers is another. Tell your lovely sister Ainsley the truth. Tell her you got pregnant, and it wasn't from a damn condom. You started screwing him right after she first had him, and you got pregnant a few months before that damn condom idea. In fact, let her know you aren't any damn few weeks. Let her know you are about seven months. Tell her you were the other woman he as with. Tell her how he was going to leave me and her for you, because he claimed to have found his soul mate in you and not her. So yeah, he told the truth when he told you he was telling me he was leaving me and you."

She looked at me and started talking like she and I were friends, "Do you believe he was gonna leave us for that bitch? I didn't take it that well. How you feel about it?"

When I did not say a word, Hadley looked back at my twin to say, "Go on. Finish telling her. This should be good."

My sister was silent as she hung her head. I would not have believed Hadley if she hadn't said it in front of Paisley. There was no way my dear sister could have done such a deed to me, but she did. Hadley waited a few more minutes and still Paisley was quiet. This man's wife casually said, "Oh, well."

She added more bullets to the gun and shot my twin in the head four times. I could not look. The brightness of the knife blade caught my eye as she removed it from her other pocket. Walking carefully, this monster walked over to my twin. Paisley's eyes and mouth were open. Blood was everywhere. You could tell she was dead. Hadley stood between my twin and me so I could not see her. I cried. I could not see her but I heard the baby cry. I thought, please don't kill the baby.

"I know you want to see it, but that would be too much like right. However, I will tell you, it's a girl. Should we call her Joy because that is what we thought we had with Anthony or should we call her Faith because we wall hoped we were the only ones. Too bad. I can't have her making the mistakes her mom and aunt made."

At point blank range, the angry monster shot the baby. I jerked and jerked but re was nothing I could do. Tossing the baby behind my sons, Hadley looked at me, and said, "That's the end of that. Now back to my cheating ass husband."

Tears would not let me cry for Paisley but my heart swelled for my daughter. She deliberately made sure I did not see the baby girl I would have called Heaven because that's how my life with her husband overall was. I glanced her way and could see her brain as her head moved side to side before stopping. At this point, I did not care about him anymore. She said, "Now, he was lying to you all the time. I know he told you I left him, and yada... yada... yada, but he was lying. He knew when to get you out before I came back. For the most, I worked hard to maintain the lifestyle he enjoys so much. I told him to tell you numerous times I will sue you for alienation of affection. He said he told you and I know he did but he also gave you his version of it. I told him if he was such a good friend, he would tell you to go your way and don't look back. You either didn't listen or he didn't tell you. Anyway, you were dicked down and too far gone, but that's cool. His dick is good, and I feel the same way. I just woke up tired of him doing what he wants. I didn't need you or your sister in my marriage. There had been countless others." I glanced at her. She spoke, "Don't tell me, you thought you were his first rodeo?"

Anger was all on my face. Hadley said, "Girl you are dumb as hell. Ain't no way you actually thought you were his first affair, by how he was talking to you all the time? He actually perfected his affair by screwing your lovely twin, Ley."

My face told her I believed him. She said, "If he fed you shit you would have ate five miles of it. I see how easy it was to trick you. Your own twin did, but anyway you kept yourselves in it. I didn't give her a warning because I found out after the fact. But you, almost two years since our phone conversation, I gave you fair warnings because you had children. But no, you got smart with me and said you are to get me first. You have no idea how many bitches he has ran through, with my money. You don't know the half of the lies he's fed you. When you would not listen and you kept calling, I really became heartless. But when you started fucking him in my house and in my bed, your ass became grass! Bitch, you were starving for a life he wouldn't give you and could never give you. I only stayed because I had too much invested. He literally had nothing until I came along and provided everything to him. But you gonna wish you had paid attention to me."

She walks towards Anthony. He was dazed and unsteady. She took the tape off his mouth. Hadley leaned into him and kissed his lips. My love no more, had water in his eyes. She touched his forehead and said mockingly, "You should have told Ley, that I quit sleeping with you because I didn't trust you. Then I found out you are HIV positive."

She looked at me and laughed while saying, "Praise God, I didn't get infected, but Ley did." I wanted to faint, but she continued, "Other than my huge life insurance policy on him, I loved him. The heart wants what the heart wants, right?"

Hadley looked back at Anthony to say, "Back to you, my love. I loved you with a love far more than anyone could, but you didn't care. You didn't give a rat's ass about me or my feelings about you. There was nothing I wouldn't have done for you. I gave you everything I had, and you screwed over me every chance you had."

His wife stood up. She was glaring down at her cheating husband. Harshly, she spoke to him, "You only wanted to fuck, fuck, and fuck. This bitch, that bitch and all the other bitches, but those two bitches took the cake. You would not let Ainsley leave well enough alone. I've had it up to here with different bitches coming in and out of my marriage, causing problems and making me cry and pray. They had your nose so far open; I'm surprised you couldn't smell this shit right here brewing."

She dropped her head and wiped her eyes. She lifted her head up and spoke. "I kept being with you because I know how I felt about you. I would have been damned if I went by your feelings. Today my love, fuck your feelings and super fuck you."

This crazy woman looked at me. "You see I told him to tell you to get some new business, before I fuck you up. He either didn't tell you or you didn't have the sense God gave to realize being involved with this married man was wrong."

She shot at my thigh but missed. His loveless wife said, "Oops, I'm sorry. That bullet wasn't meant for you. It was meant for him. Let's get rid of our common denominator shall we, so the real games can begin."

No warning was given as she turned the gun towards her husband and opened fire on him. I could not believe she was shooting the man she said she loves. My emotions were all over the room. I started crying. She hollered, "Shut the hell up, bitch. Your chance coming, just hold on. I'm saving the best for last."

Anthony was indeed dead. I saw the blood coming out his mouth and from every place she shot. This vengeful woman had no pity for the man she married. I don't know what she is going to do with me. As of now, I wished she had killed me. I have witnessed those dear to me caught up in my sin. They paid with their lives because of my wants. I cried and jerked on the chains but could not get loose.

She gave me a smile of peace as she spoke calmly, "I warned you but let me tell you a few things first. My mother was dying of cancer, and I took time to be with her. My husband. God bless his soul; didn't want my mother living with us. I took it upon myself and moved to her. He didn't want to come because he claims he has work to do. Trust me, he was doing work, but I wasn't getting paid for it."

Hadley stops talking. She walked closer to me and slapped me so hard; my body shook in the chains with unbelievable force. As I looked at her with nothing left to lose, she became cocky. "I have saved judges, policemen, lawyers and countless of civilians. None of them would convict me. In fact, this would be a crime of passion but not my passion. You done fucked up now. You have messed around with the wrong woman's husband and to think he had yo stank ass in my bed, driving my car and acting like you were better than me. Bitch you deserve to die. But I must give it to you. Ainsley, you are a cool ass snake. You just hissed at the wrong damn thing."

She was delighting herself in this. I looked over at my love's lifeless body. She asked me with amazement, "You didn't think I would kill my own husband, did you?"

I could not say a word, so she said, "You aren't going to die today! Thank God for that. I have a heart. I had a better heart, but you helped him break it. You could not leave well enough alone. You had to have the one dick that belonged to the wrong woman. All your life you searched and searched for what the hell ever for; just to end up looking like a damn fool. You had enough problems going on with your health, but you included my husband. You couldn't just be his friend and let that shit ride. You had to be riding with him and on him. I get it; you had a rough go at life. Because I am a doctor and I like helping people, I'm gonna help you. In fact, you will spend the rest of your life thinking about this painful night and why you did it."

My eyes bucked as she said it again. "That's right. Why you did it? Remember this is your crime of passion and the jury will see it like this. You killed your sister for getting pregnant by the man you love. You killed the baby because it was not yours. You killed your children to make it look like a robbery gone badly, mainly because they saw you kill their TT and Uncle Ant. You almost killed me because I was the only thing standing in your way with my husband, but you didn't hit a main artery. You in your distraught state, missed. You passed out before you could kill yourself."

I didn't know what to think of what she was saying to me. She smiled and said, "To be honest, I really wanted Christ to have his way but HE in my opinion was taking too long. I decided to help things along the way. Make you see how it feels to know the one you love doesn't love you. You needed to see first-hand what it's like to be in a loveless relationship after finding what you called love. Don't worry you won't be like this when they come for you."

She reached in her lower scrub pants pocket. I don't know what she got, but she gave me a shot in my leg. She said, "This is an untraceable drug. You are about to blank out from the pain and anger you just witnessed. You won't remember, but you will remember pulling this trigger. When you awake, your life as you know it will be no more. You will wish you had of listened to me and stayed out my business, and out of my damn marriage.

Warning comes before destruction and you let another's woman dick, fuck you up for life. Oh well. That's the choice you made. Deal with it. Goodnight."

I lifted my head and noticed how Hadley was becoming blurry. I tried shaking my head to see more of her, but I heard her laughter as she spoke candidly, "I'll see you in court, you diabetic bitch."

EPILOGUE

Hadley went on about her life but her conscience bothered her for what she did. Ainsley didn't believe she killed her family but could not prove she didn't do it, although she felt Hadley committed the murders.

At trial, Hadley spoke on her behalf stating she was delusional and need psychotic help. The judge declared Ainsley insane and received a lesser crime for her inability to stand trial. She was sentenced fifty years in a deranged halfway house, twenty years suspended.

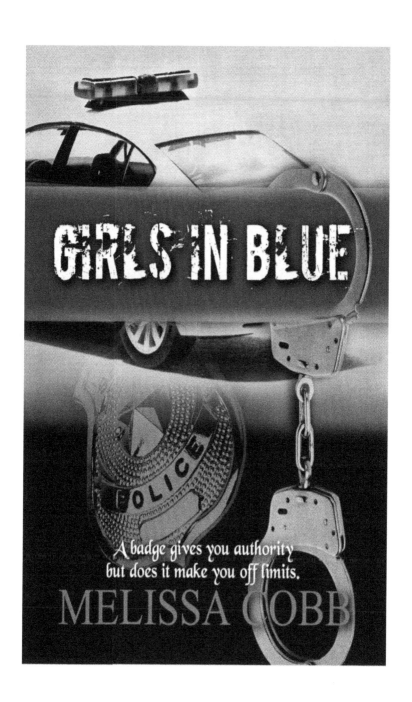

GIRLS IN BLUE

A badge gives you authority
but does it make you off limits.

MELISSA COBB

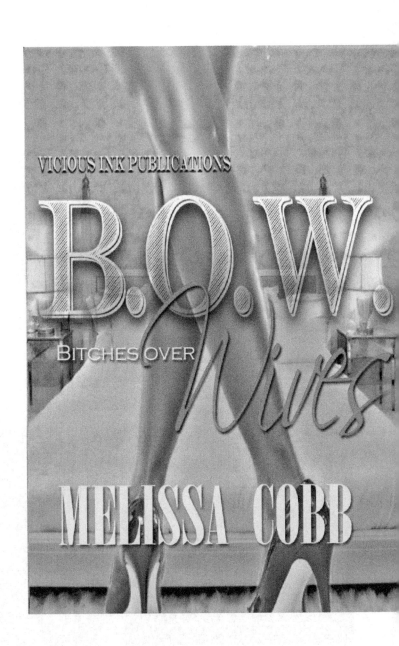

VICIOUS INK PUBLICATIONS

B.O.W.

BITCHES OVER *Wives*

MELISSA COBB

Made in the USA
Columbia, SC
10 April 2023